THE ACE OF SPADES MURDER

ALSO BY HARRY STEPHEN KEELER

The "Screwball Circus" Mysteries:

The Vanishing Gold Truck
The Ace of Spades Murder
The Case of the Jeweled Ragpicker
Stand By—London Calling!
The Case of the Crazy Corpse
The Circus Stealers
A Copy of Beowulf
Report on Vanessa Hewstone
The Six from Nowhere

The "Way Out" Series

The Peacock Fan
The Sharkskin Book
The Book with Orange Leaves
Two Strange Ladies
The Case of 16 Beans

Others Novels

The Amazing Web
The Box from Japan
The Case of the Ivory Arrow
The Case of the Mysterious Moll
The Case of the Transparent Nude
The Case of the Transposed Legs
The Face of the Man from Saturn
Find the Clock
The Five Silver Buddhas
The Fourth King
The Green Jade Hand
Hangman's Nights
The Iron Ring
The Man Who Changed His Skin
The Monocled Monster
The Murder of London Lew
The Mystery of the Fiddling Cracksman
Riddle of the Travelling Skull
The Search for X-Y-Z
Sing Sing Nights
The Spectacles of Mr. Cagliostro
Thieves' Nights

THE ACE OF SPADES MURDER

HARRY STEPHEN KEELER

The Screwball Circus Mysteries #2

WILDSIDE PRESS

CHAPTER I

UNFOLDING OF AN ENIGMA!

Detective Sergeant Frank DuShane, temporarily assigned as ordinary plainclothes-man to the Depot-View Police Station, on the down-at-heel south fringe of Chicago's great downtown district, was just about to go off duty for the night—it being now 10 minutes after 6 in the morning!—when the telephone call came on the regular station phone, standing on the shiny wicket ledge presided over by the big blue-uniformed, brass-buttoned, white-moustached day station-sergeant, who droned out: "Somebody wants *you*, Frank, pers'nally." DuShane, himself behind the wallboard partition that held the booking wicket and at the same time cut off the front tall-windowed section of the station from the rest of the big whitewashed room, was at this moment in the act of fixing up his appearance preparatory to going off duty. A procedure which involved very little inasmuch as he had been assigned to this station as special plainclothesman to conduct a very special investigation in this particular police area. He leisurely completed his beautification process by carefully depositing back on his thinning hair his black derby hat, meticulously arranging its exact set and angle, and then only turning and strolling across the wood-floored space between himself and the phone, and casually picking up the instrument. "DuShane talking," he said.

"I—I sure *am* glad I catch you," returned a voice in which there was great relief of tone, coupled with a slight but definite thickness of utterance that betrayed the speaker clearly to be a German Jew. "I was so afraid you had already, maybe yes, started for home, and—"

"Well, I ain't," assured DuShane. "As you can roughly figger out—since I'm right on this here wire." And added irritably: "And so now—who the hell's talking, anyway?"

"Well, this is Hyman Silver, Mister—DuShane. Propri'tor of the Hotel Romanorum—on West Pres'dent Street—you maybe know the hotel?"

"Well," returned DuShane, "I know the dump—by sight. For I certain'y been past it often enough with other detectives—partic'ly while assigned here from the Bureau. And heard a good deal about it—from them that know. You're today a no-questions-asked hotel! Yes, no? For I saw a heav'y-veiled, wealthy-lookin' woman—Glencoe or Winetka stuff, if anything—maybe Beverly Hills stuff so far's that goes—and a wealthy-lookin' man—Lake Front Drive stuff, *him*—comin' down t'gether, the other day—and without baggage!—them marble stairs that lead from your second floor—your first room-floor, that is—to your side entrance there on Canyon Street, well back o' Pres'dent by the whole depth of your place. And saw 'em get into different cabs—both of 'em!—out on Pres'dent Street. Ain't you afraid, Silver," DuShane now taunted, "that in maintainin' a side stairway, 'way off from your foyer and main stairway, people—will beat their bills?"

Hyman Silver, proprietor of the Hotel Romanorum, gave a humourless laugh. "Well, Mr. DuShane, I admit that the highbrow that built this hotel didn't know Human Nature. But we don't worry here about that side-street exit at all. This is a strictly cash-in-advance place. And anybody who wants to 'out' by the side entrance on narrow Canyon Street can go that way."

"Well, what's on your mind, Silver?"

"Mr. DuShane," the hotel proprietor said, "somep'n' was fetched into my hotel last night. And depos'ted—in one of the rooms what's on my first room-floor—the second floor, of course. And the thing that was planted on me in the night was—a human body."

"A body?" ejaculated DuShane. "Well, where the hell was you?—or your all-night room-clerk? Fetched in, this body, you mean, by that same side stairway we been talking about? If so—"

"No, Mr. DuShane. Them what fetched it into my place maybe went out that way—I wouldn't know—but they fetched it up and in by way of the firescape—on the west or alley side. The reason I know is that the swinging, counterweighted stairway o' the firescape is down this morning. To the ground. And a long 8-foot len'th of stiff, heavy wire, with a bent hook on the end, is still 'ttached to it, showin' they reached up in the dark and pulled it down. And the window of this room was way up. And—"

"Any persons in rooms whose windows open near the firescape—to the sides or above?—hear any of all this firescape lugging?" inquired DuShane, still a bit sceptical about this unusual incident. "Though I suppose," he now added, in fairness, "it *is* too early to've inquired."

"Wasn't any rooms rented on that side of the house, Mr. DuShane," returned the proprietor lugubriously. "They're hotter'n hell in summer. We rent from the street sides first—then start in on the alley side. We never got full up so far as even the alley side, up to any part of last night."

"Oh yeah, I see. No witnesses, then, to sights, sounds, nor gruntings? Well, I guess the long hooked wire, and the firescape stairway down on the ground, tell the facts pretty well. The ingress. So—go on with your tale?"

"Yes, Mr. DuShane. Well, how they went out after they fetched the body in, I wouldn't, as I say, know. Maybe they—they just went back down the firescape, and rejoined the car what brought 'em here: or maybe, again, they went out by that side entrance of ours, and rejoined the car up street or somethin'—I just wouldn't know, either. For—"

"How in hell," demanded DuShane helplessly, "do you know a car even brought *them*—whoever *they* are?"

"I don't know nothing, Mr. DuShane. Other than that a big fine car, Rolls-Royce-like, slithered out the alley mouth last night, at around 10 o'clock or so, wound past the front o' the hotel, and dis'ppeared. Where, I wouldn't know. I didn't even see all this. My night-man mentioned it, that's all."

"Well, what kind of a body was it? Some medical-school stiff—maybe? Or—or some hit-and-run victim from the alley itself?"

"No, Mr. DuShane. It—it was a murdered man."

"Oh-oh! Shot somewhere, eh?"

"No, Mr. DuShane. It's the body of a man who ain't nothing less than a—a ragpicker! He's a black Negro, 'bout 30 years old, ragged and dirty. Wearing different shoes each foot, a high one and a low one. No socks at all. The high black shoe is laced with twine. The other one, a tan oxford, held together only with a rusty—a rusty paper-clip! Burlap pants—"

"Burlap—pants? For the love o'—"

"Yes, Mr. DuShane, and hand made—for they're sewed with coarse, dirty, once-white grocer's string. And he's wearing a filthy tattered shirt so black that—well, it's obvious it ain't been changed for months. In fact, when you put your nose close to it—it smells of garbage. His nails is just bulging with dirt and ashes and—"

"Ashes, eh? Ragpicker type, all right. Go on?"

"—and he's even wearing a belt to hold up his burlap pants that's nothin' but a len'th of—of clothesline."

"I see. That is, I see like a bat under a thousand-watt lamp. For a body such as you describe is enough to suggest that a hotel where it's found is nothing but a dump—but all right. Well, it seems to me, Silver, that this is just a routine affair, no matter how it looks to *you*. So I'll make a report to the station-sarge here when he gets back to his stool—and before *I* go off duty—I'm going off now, you know. Maybe," he ventured, but ironically, "McCrearity may even be able to figure out *why* they lugged the body into your place!"

"Mr. DuShane," Silver begged fervently, "don't turn this over—to your station chief. He's—he's a hard man, that McCrearity—with a rep'tation for arresting ever'body connected with a—you see," he added lamely, "you was pointed out to me the other day as an off'cer who'd been on the Hom'cide Detail at the Detective Bureau in your day—rather, as a p'lice invest'gator who didn't—didn't go haywire in a killing, and suspect ever'body about, as havin' somethin' to do with it. And accusin' ever'body, bar none, of lying like hell. And of concealing clues. And—and whatnot. The party said you had lots of exper'ence—in strange murders. So won't you come over yourself—and take over—first of all? For this murder," finished Mr. Silver, like a man playing a high trump, "contains an angle so—so damned strange, that it'll—it'll knock you for a row. For two rows, Mr. DuShane. In short, you may think you've just heard about a simple case of a black ragpicker, bumped off and dumped on to a decent hotel. But you—you ain't heard nothing yet. Nothing, see? So will you come?"

CHAPTER II

HOTEL ROMANORUM

DuShane, having hung promptly and immediately up, was just unlimbering his blue-serge-clad shank from the stool as McCrearity, the white-moustached station-sergeant, returned and unlocked himself clatteringly, by his key, back into the partitioned front office.

"I'm not checking out yet, Sarge," DuShane said. "That is—consider me still—on duty. Right? For I'm making a call over at the old Hotel Romanorum. Proprietor over there—hrmph—wants me to pers'nally look into something."

"Okay, Frank. Hope you get something out of it that'll make the Bureau leave you here a few days longer. But you don't need to report back if there's nothing to what you're looking into. If I don't hear anything from you in an hour, I'll set you down myself on the record-sheet as 'out and went home.'"

"Thanks, Sarge."

Outside, on the single stone doorstep of Depot-View Police Station, DuShane stood for a second or two, gratefully breathing in the now fresh-smelling, sun-lighted air of which he'd been getting so little in his recent night work; then he stepped almost reluctantly down on the sidewalk, and strode northward.

A walk of a long block in that direction and he stood in front of the Hotel Romanorum itself, gazing querulously upward at its scant 3 stories. Hopelessly down and out was it today, its brown stone, once perhaps aristocratic, chipped and eaten badly by the acid smoke-soaked rains of Chicago. DuShane had only to step up two low steps off the sidewalk to find himself in the hotel itself, containing a practically lobbyless lobby—because of the ground-floor area consumed by the restaurant.

Beyond the very threshold of the entrance—and to the right thereof—rose a broad marble stairway with hand-chiselled busts of no-doubt-once-famous Roman orators set immobilely in niches alongside it. Immediately beyond the base of the marble stairway, and hence also to the right, was a narrow splintered wooden counter, doubtlessly no part of the original hotel at all, with a prosaic-looking tin-framed electric light pouring down on a

register book on it. Behind the short counter, morosely and patiently waiting, no doubt, was a bald-headed man of about 40, in flamboyantly-flowered
shirt-sleeves; he had thick lips, black eyes, and a great beak of a nose. At the
low door of a room a half-dozen feet back of the counter, hand on the knob
as though zealously guarding it, stood a middle-aged but strong-looking
woman in black work clothes, a canvas apron over her front, and a bunch
of keys at her waist. Evidently the housekeeper. She looked not just ill at
ease—but almost ill!

"I'm Hyman Silver, of course," the man behind the counter was assur-
ing DuShane. "Glad you got here, Inspec—Mr. DuShane. This here lady
now is my housekeeper—Mrs. Spewack—Mrs. Eva Spewack. And *him*—
well, we got him in there—in the office room."

"You should ought to have left him in the room where he was found—
oh, all right," DuShane broke off. He turned curtly, and, at the counter's
end, turned again and threaded his way through the narrow gap between it
and the stand-up switchboard beyond, even as Hyman Silver himself, reaching the door first, swung it partly open. DuShane was already stepping in
through the partial opening, followed by the proprietor. And the woman,
now bulwarked, as it were, by two husky men, was filing in, too, even closing the door softly but firmly behind them all.

And now DuShane, well inside—and disregarding a sheet-draped structure of chairs which had been set up near a generously-sized and apparently
south-facing window to his left—cast a hasty, supercilious, and appraising
glance about this carpetless, low-ceilinged room in which—*if* he took charge
of this ridiculous affair—he would have to hold forth, in a little while, to
reporters and cameramen probably itching to write it up facetiously. Him,
included! For DuShane was rapidly becoming more and more certain—had
been, even on the way over—and chiefly because the unsavoury description
of the dead man made it practically impossible he could have been a lure-
victim—DuShane was becoming certain now, despite even the promise of
so-called "angles," that this whole affair was nothing more than the matter
of a "hit-and-run" auto-victim, with skull partly bashed in by a front wheel,
struck down either in the alley close by or elsewhere in the city, but shoved,
for purposes of petty revenge or perhaps concealment of the accident itself,
into the window of a cheap hotel.

"I'll—I'll be damned," he muttered—though to himself alone, "if I'll
have anything to do with this fool case. Outside of hearing these people's
say-so's, and then slithering-to-hell out o' here. I'll—I'll have nothing to
do with it. Angles or no angles. I won't—so help me Hannah!" Indeed, to
DuShane, who in his day had taken charge of the investigations of the murders of a multi-millionaire, a famous author, and a world-beauty of an actress, holding forth to reporters on those occasions in, respectively, a rich

bust-studded library, a writing nook with gold typewriter and lithographs of its owner's past successful motion-pictures on the walls, and an incense-drenched boudoir with silken hangings, this room was no place—no-o-o-o place at all!—for a self-respecting crime investigator to be even snapped in or against!

He turned irritably to the woman, who stood patiently behind him.

"Okay, if you're the official sheet-yanker around here! You can now yank away, Mrs.—Mrs.—Mrs.—"

"Spewack is the name, sir," the woman said.

But it was Silver, the hotel proprietor, who had taken charge of the "sheet-yanking" on DuShane's order thereto. He had, with a pull, and a vigorous rolling-up motion of his forearms, removed a great soiled double-bed-width sheet that had covered it all, revealing dramatically, thereby, the body of the presumed black ragpicker—auto-victim, as DuShane was certain he was—laid out, black face and front of body upward, on 6 chairs, obviously lobby chairs, oddly arranged with their backs outward, the fronts of their seats some 6 or 7 inches from each other, like an improvised bier with a protective railing! And DuShane, by now behind the midmost of the three chairs making the outside of the improvised bier, his forearms resting idly on its back, stood looking down on the thing, laid out on the seats thereof.

And DuShane's nostrils contracted.

Fooey!

For the dead man was indeed all that Silver had described him to be. Black as coal, an Afro-American almost entirely without white blood, as were so many Negroes today in America. Ragpicker all right, DuShane could not help but completely agree, and without having even to see ashes under the man's nails, for the latter not only carried a three- or four-day growth of stubble on his black face, but his clothes were exactly as Hyman Silver had set forth. Now the woman designated by the proprietor as his housekeeper, and standing behind the two men, spoke:

"There he was, Inspector, when I went into the mop and broom room— at least as we call it—this morning, on the floor above and 'way back. Lying crumpled on his face by the wide-opened window. And—oh my!—I came down and brought up Mr. Silver at once. And together we—"

"Bringin' up Silver was a'right," DuShane said sternly. "But you shouldn't have helped him disturb the body. But *I* got my own theories about this little affair as you can both see—well, I'm a hom'cide spec'list—not a—a—a dabbler in manslaughter. I'm—"

"But it isn't—manslaughter, Inspector," the woman protested. "Mr. Silver wouldn't have called you—had it been manslaughter. Or—or palpably such. For it's a case of a man who's—but here!—it's—it's hardly up to *me* to be—to be interpolating *my* remarks in an affair which is strictly between you and Mr. Silver only. However—it wasn't manslaughter."

"Says on'y him and you, Mrs.—Mrs.—Mrs.—"

"Spewack is the name, Inspector. Who struck him down, and why, may never be known to any of us three, but may heaven forfend that any of us, now in this sordid chamber, ever attain the poor wretch's fate. For he—"

"May heaven forfend we don't!" agreed DuShane dryly. "Meaning—'at we don't all three of us wind up wearin' home-sewed burlappy pants! For he's just a case of a dingo who didn't jump fast enough out of an auto headlight, and—He had turned to the woman. "You b'en in show-business, ain't you, Mrs.—Mrs.—"

"Yes," nodded the woman humbly. "I travelled for many years with Captain Billy Benziger's stock troupe. Yes, Inspector, I may be today but Mrs. Eva Spewack, hotel housekeeper; but I'm also Mrs. Eva Spewack from out the golden, halcyon days of true thespianism."

"And s'pose," put in DuShane peremptorily, and with a sudden glance at his watch, "that we all leave our halcyonish gold-plated pasts—all of us!—and get back to our tarnished, nickel-plated presents? Okay—ever'body?"

"O—kay!" came promptly from Hyman Silver.

"Well, s'pose, Silver, first of all," the detective-sergeant said, "'at since I'm in a sort of minor'ty of one ag'in two around here, that this here 'unsavoury rose by any name' is a hit-and-run victim—just s'pose we disregard a-a-all that, and get down to brass tacks: namely, the on'y part of this affair that we really *do* know somep'n about. In short—that you—or the Hotel Romanorum—caught the corpse un-delicious. Are you on duty yourself here any part of the night?"

Silver opened his mouth as though to expostulate about something. Then, raising his hands in a curious, futile, almost pawnbrokerlike gesture, he answered DuShane.

"No," he said, "I ain't. A night man with one leg—he uses a crutch—an Englishman he is, named Titcomb. He handles the desk contin'ously from 8 P.M. to 8 next morning. But Tit had said he wanted off this morning, so I come on early, see? At 5. I—I don't pay much salary around here, y'know, and I got to help the help out when they ask favours. Mrs. Spewack here I've often helped out by—"

"Well, Tit Esquire'll have to be contacted, of course," broke in DuShane, "by somebody—by whoever officially follows this here affair up—and the fact elic'ted, *not* that Rolls-Royces slithered out of the alley in the night, but whether he heard *anything* in the night, in the dark courtway there." And he inclined his head courtway ward.

"Tit keeps to his stool all night," said Silver, shaking his head. "Except for catching a breath in the front door, now and then. He don't even—with his crutch—try to take folks to their rooms. He tells 'em how to reach their rooms, by the good big numbers we got on the doors. What drowsing he does, he does out there. I've—I've warned him about sneaking in here to sleep on the couch. He don't even come in here in the night except maybe to lock some guest's val'bles in the safe yonder—but damn few of our guests ever have val'bles to lock up. None at least last night, anyway, as shown on the reg'ster."

"I'll bet they don't!" nodded DuShane sagely.

"In fact, I'll bet most o' *your* guests, Silver, just about own the shirts on their backs and their night's room rent, and no more. Well, that's that, then."

He turned to the woman.

"And now for you. Since you're the official finder of this black corpse, just what did you do, may I ask—when you did find him? Walked in on him, that is, all by your lonesome? Search him?"

"You're joking of course, Inspector," the woman retorted painedly. "I'd only come into the hotel two or three minutes before, at most—had but only within about two minutes or so said good morning to Mr. Silver here, on my way through the lobby and upstairs to the top floor where my locker is, when I came down a flight and went straight to that broom room. And walking in as I did on this black body—and all within 3 minutes or so of having come into the hotel—well, I just stood paralysed in my tracks. Seeing, that is, *all* that I saw! Then I fled right downstairs and called Mr. Silver up—and when *he* saw all that I saw—we were, within short order—after, that is, Mr. Silver had made a bit more of an examination than I had—we were lugging—half sliding, at times—the black man down here. Oh dear—awful!"

"Awful," agreed DuShane critically, "yes. That the two of you, in moving the body, may have kicked aside some cuff-link or somethin' dropped in that mop room upstairs by them as laid this black egg there. But the room c'n be looked over later easy enough. And the firescape, too—though if the stairway of it's down on the ground—in fact, I c'n see that myself from here—and there's a hooked reaching-wire attached to it—it pretty much tells about all the tale *it* can. Except as to where in yonder alley"—he tossed his derby-hatted head in that direction—"this Senegamblin' man got goosed by that Rolls-Royce or what—or where in the whole damned city. For the city's puh-lenty big! And a corpse *can* be carried about in a Rolls-Royce—a Ford coupy—or a Whippet." He looked down at the body again. "Money?" He shook his head almost amusedly. "I bet he ain't a red penny on him."

"Right!" said Silver triumphantly. "For I searched him immediat—oh, in front of Mrs. Spewack here, o' course, as a witness—sure. I searched the on'y pockets this fellow had. Them burlap pants ones. But not a penny on or in 'em. Nor a box of—or paper of—matches. Just them"—and he now tossed his head toward the open rolltop desk where lay many playing-cards, face up—"just them cards—in a pack—in his hip pocket."

DuShane stepped over, picked one up. It was one of a deck so old that the edges of all in it had been worn, some ragged, some even frayed. The design on the shiny backs had partly worn away on some. On the faces of some, certain pips themselves had disappeared from countless abradings.

"These here are the pasteboards," he observed dryly, "that Noah used on the ark, I guess. Waiting for the water to subside." He shook his head. "You'd think a ragpicker'd keep some of the nice deluxey things he picks up in the dumps; but no, he's got to sell ever'thing, and—" He turned to Silver, puzzledly. "Was you trying to while away your suspense while I was coming here—dealing yourself a bit o' solitaire?"

"Gee no! I—I had been exam'ning the cards. To see—how many. That is, to see if one card—a card—a certain card was missing. For—"

"Missing? What the hell you mean? Why should a card—be missing—in this ragpicker's deck? *Was* there any missing?"

"Oh yes, there was. As I suspected there might—yes, there was. When I found, by count, only 51. And searched. Yes, the Ace o' Spades—*it's* missing, all right. It's missing!"

"It prob'ly wore out, a year or so back," grunted DuShane. "For even in a one-hoss shay, schedoodled to go to pieces all t'gether, somethin's got to wear out first. In this case—phooey on it."

And he came disgruntledly back to the body, and the ever gloomy hotel proprietor.

"Well, Silver," the detective-sergeant said, "since you've seen all sides of this corpse undelicious—front side—back side—enough to pluck cards out of the hip pocket on that side—I have to p'esume you're sure 'at you didn't see a bashed-in skull. Did you?" He fastened baleful glare on the proprietor. "For if you didn't—if you merely assumed somebody swung on him with a blackjack or a piece o' pipe just because he happens to be dead and—well, has it ever occurred to any of you around here that maybe he just dropped somewhere in his tracks?—from ticker-disease?"

"He didn't die of no heart disease," retorted Silver emphatically. "Nor was he shot, as I told you. Nor was he even clouted. I—I never said he had a bashed-in skull."

"Just dead, eh?" said DuShane scornfully, with a mirthless smile. "Not shot, nor bashed—nor dead from ticker-stoppage—and ever'body around here u-nanny-mous thereto. Well just how now," he inquired, throwing his gaze alternately to each side of him to show he was addressing everybody involved, "do you know all this, Doctor Silver and—Doctor—Doctor—uh—ah—"

"'Doctor' Spewack is what you want to facetiously call me," the woman said with dignity. "Except that, of course, I'm not a doctor. But it isn't fair to Mr. Silver here to impute that he doesn't know—"

"To answer your question, Mr. DuShane," put in Silver, with sudden fierceness, "I—I suggest we turn this feller over. That is, will you help me to? You take his feet and knees, Mr. DuShane, and I'll take the shoulders, yes? And together we'll sort o'—o' roll him gently over on to the seats of them far chairs."

And without even waiting for DuShane's grumpy assent, Silver went lumberingly around to the head of the improvised bier-supported body. Whereupon DuShane, glad to at least get *somewhere* in this hazy riddle, repaired over to the feet and knees end of the corpse. Noting again, as he did so, and still puzzledly, how those chair fronts were all of 5 inches apart! Now the two men prepared to take hold together. But DuShane stayed operations for a second, by raising a hand.

"I may's well tell you here and now, Silver," he announced sternly, almost chidingly, "that I ain't going to take over your case—even though, being a detective-sergeant, and on a detail at th' Bureau 'at handles such things as found dead cuckoos, and bein' first on the scene here, to boot—offic'lly, that is—I've the right to. And could. But take over I ain't going to, see? For I don't want my perfessional name assoc'ated with no crim'logical cases so petty like—like dirty ragpickers, that prob'ly on'y died anyway from ptomaines or somethin' they et out of a garbage heap, dumped into down-at-heel hotels. 'Twouldn't be fittin' for the name of DuShane, even in the p'lice records. O—kay. Let's turn."

Hyman Silver took hold tightly of the black shoulders in front of him. As did DuShane, at his own end, of the shinbones and knees, of the bier-supported corpse. Now, by torque applied in the same direction, and at the same time, and on a body that was partially rigid already, they rolled it—rather, practically flopped it—over till it lay face downward on the further three chair seats. And now, indeed, was revealed plainly why—the gap between the chairs! And now was revealed furthermore, and conclusively, why this black victim had *not* met his death from heart-failure, nor shooting, nor a host of other simple things.

For, protruding from his filthily-shirted back—though through a bright, shiny, brand-new gilt-edged Ace of Spades, face out, which it had spitted— was a jewelled-handled dagger, sunk hilt deep; a dagger, the yellow metal of whose hilt and handle, and the blazing scintillations from which handle, in the beam of bright sunlight falling full on it at this second, almost in themselves betrayed what DuShane himself was destined, in less than 2 more hours, to learn from an expert.

Namely, that the dagger's hilt and handle were of solid gold; and that the handle was studded with small, though genuine diamonds and rubies and emeralds; and that the weapon was worth, at most conservative estimate, $25,000!

But DuShane, gazing dumbly down at those blazing rainbow-hued scintillations—that brand-new Ace of Spades which the dagger had spitted, pinned, anchored, to the black shirted back—casting even a single, almost fearful, glance sidewise of himself across the room to that Ace-of-Spadeless pack of worn cards lying over on the rolltop desk—was not even thinking, at this second, so far ahead as experts in jewels and precious metals. Instead, he was making single grim comment.

"I'll tell the cock-eyed world, Silver, that you got a murder—a little off the beam! Ve-e-e-ry much so—*and* how! All right, then. Where's your phone? Trot me it out. So's I can get the Bureau. We'll need photographers, finger-print men, moulage experts—The Works!—"

"You—you mean," said Hyman Silver, almost pitiously unbelievingly, "that you'll take over the case—yourself? And—and—and solve it?"

"I mean," said Frank DuShane, professional criminologist, "'at I'll take over the case, yes. Though whether I solve it or not, is somethin' that nobody in the world can say—right now. But whether I *do*—or whether I *don't*—one thing *is* cert: a hunderd p'cent cert. And here 'tis, Silver." DuShane paused but a second, but impressively. "With this here case such as it is—and with no less'n 25 true-crime-myst'ry mags in the field, and thousands more to get issued durin' future years—we're—we're all destined, Silver, to go down in hist'ry. Me, you—and even Mrs. Beeswax!"

CHAPTER III

"SPOT GIRL"

Angus MacWhorter, owner and proprietor of MacWhorter's Mammoth Motorized Shows, touring America's great Southwest, did not realize, as he sat in his personal trailer, a full hour after the close of the evening's show, reading his nightly chapter from his great morocco-bound Bible, what an incongruous picture he presented.

For he was still in his ringmaster's costume, with tall silk hat even now absent-mindedly atop his long-faced head with its high grey-touched sideburns; and with his long-tailed black swallowtail coat, he looked like nothing so much as a great, gaunt, time-ridden crow of some sort. Particularly so under the brilliant light emanating from the powerful brass oil-lamp in the trailer's ceiling, which, focusing down on the small portable table carrying the huge Bible, and lighting up the few scant additional pieces of ascetic furniture the trailer contained, brought out the sad and brooding countenance of MacWhorter, the seams in his great face.

Now came a timid tap on the door of the trailer. MacWhorter, huge finger on a passage, looked up.

"Come in," he called.

It was, beyond any doubt, he realized, Karl the Klown, returning for his magazine which he'd agitatedly left on the table, 5 minutes or so before, after having received from his employer a stiff lecture on the evils of drinking. Indeed, the gaudy magazine which Karl the Klown had apologetically mentioned having picked up in town this very evening before the show, for lack of anything better obtainable, lay on the table now awaiting the clown's return, its title staring across the table in brilliant yellow letters outlined in black, reading *Famous Unsolved Crime Mysteries* and with, lower down on it, boxed, a screaming announcement which read:

In this Issue
THE RAGPICKER JOE MURDER
of 25 years ago
and
13 other famous unsolved crimes.

The magazine's cover picture, done in apparently all the colours of the rainbow, was evidently—as perhaps even one might surmise—a picturization of the Ragpicker Joe Murder, and none of the other 13!—for it showed a raggedly-shirted back, surmounted by an ebony black neck, from which back protruded, through an Ace of Spades face upward, a jewelled dagger handle.

But MacWhorter was not engaged just now, close on to midnight of this pleasant day of June the 4th, in making critical reflections of any sort upon the kind of reading his chief clown was indulging in. Instead, he was gazing toward the trailer door. For not Karl, but a girl was coming in, her petite body rising slightly as she ascended the two topmost steps of the short flight leading upward to the trailer door. Once in, moreover, she immediately closed the trailer door behind her. She was about 21 years of age, and was clad in a most curious—perhaps in some ways scant, too!—costume suggesting, beyond any doubt whatsoever, "Autumn," for its short skirt and bodice appeared to be a bewildering congeries of nut-brown autumn leaves carelessly whisked together as though by some errant whimsical wind. It was a costume, no less, which, in the MacWhorter Shows, was known as a "spot girl costume." Its wearer was spot girl! One of those natural beauties who wear pretty costumes, perhaps a bit scant, perhaps not, to light up a show with youth, beauty, even sex.

Her costume of nut-brown leaves matched exactly the tender brown eyes in her oval face. A little cap, rather a huge oak leaf, was on her brown tresses. And the bare limbs—at least such as showed from the tops of her autumn-brown socks to the bottom of the short leaf-skirt, were ivory like, blemishless, perfect as though moulded. She was sex, in all degrees, yet about her was not the slightest hint of the hardness of, say, the typical circus-rider, or the platform dancing-girl.

She spoke, hand still on inner knob of trailer door:

"You wished to see me, Mr. MacWhorter?"

"Yes, Melody," said the circus proprietor. "I did. That's why I asked Big Dolly—to send you over. I'm—well, I'm terribly worried about you, Melody. Here—sit over here, won't you, my dear, across from me?"

He extended a great tree-trunk of an arm across the tiny table and removed, from the opposite side of it to a side adjoining him, where it had partly perhaps blocked the use of a small folding chair whose back was hardly more than tabletop high, his loaded blackthorn cane. The girl came across the scant bit of space intervening between table and trailer door, and dropped down into the folding chair. She sighed heavily, resting her eyes unseeingly on MacWhorter's silk hat. Which made him suddenly come to himself.

"Heaven—bless me!" he said. "Here I sit—with my hat on—before a lady." He whisked it off, and stood it temporarily upmost on the floor. "Yes, I wear it with no compunction when reading my Bible. The Lord doesn't subscribe to etiquette. That's man's invention!"

She did not even smile at the quaint concept. His gaze grew troubled.

"Yes, Melody," he now repeated, "I sent for you, yes. For I'm worried about you. Worried, my dear. I—I want to know what on earth's happened to you? What's gone wrong? For in the course of no more than—well, 48 hours—you've changed from a laughing, happy girl to one so sad—so sad that—"

"It's nothing, Mr. MacWhorter." There was no assurance in her voice, however.

"Is it," he persisted, "anything—about Bill Chattock? Who asked for an indefinite leave yesterday morning—that is, a leave not to exceed two weeks? To transact some business in Chicago? That was kind of odd, considering—wasn't it?"

"No." Her answer was as toneless as all her previous responses.

And almost as though to change a painful subject, she reached out and picked up the magazine left by Karl the Klown.

"Would you drop that off at Karl's?" he asked. "It may save him from going on a drunk tonight, probably, as a result of my lecturing him against drinking." He paused. "Is there something about that magazine—or its publisher—that hurts you deeply?"

"No." But she seemed to realize that her answer was belied by her still-lingering expression. "1 guess I—I was thinking of—well, that Bill Chattock thinks that, amongst several things he expects to accomplish on his leave of absence, one will be the solution of that mystery—yes, the very one depicted here."

"Well, that would give you and him a nest-egg," said MacWhorter. "But how, may I ask, does Bill expect to bring back a solution of a case that's apparently gone down amongst the unsolvable cases of crime?"

"By stopping at the same hotel in Chicago where it happened, I guess," said the girl wearily.

"25 long years—after?" Even MacWhorter had to shake his head at this. "For even a line there reads 'of 25 years ago,' and—well, this *does* get us around to Bill. Rather, the fact that you and he apparently *haven't* had a tiff. For I did think, my dear, that this sudden terrible sadness of Melody Ashbrooke was the result of no less than a foolish tiff with Bill Chattock. And that—but maybe it is. Is it?" She made no answer. 'For it's been a sort of dream of mine—a wish of an old man trying to play Destiny!—that Bill Chattock, whom I took out of a dark, lightless, unhealthy winery cellar laboratory where he was analysing wines and badly needing a healthful year in the open, and which I could give him—*and* the little girl I looked up in Omaha just because her name was Melody, and found to be indeed the daughter of the man who—"

"Oh, how I wish," the girl put in impulsively, her hitherto toneless voice suffused for the first time with some intense emotion, "that you had known my mother, too. For then—then you could give me a sort of inside slant on her—as to whether—whether—uh—ah—"

"Alas, child," MacWhorter put in, "when I knew your father, you weren't even a gleam of adoration in his eyes, nor the woman he had not even yet met! Yes, your mother. No, child, when I knew your father last you were just a curious dream in his poetic mind—a dream that *if* he ever had a little daughter—through meeting up with the desirable mother for said daughter!—he was going to name her Melody. And so, when years later—same being 3 months ago!—I passed through Maysville, Nebraska, just south of Omaha, and saw in an Omaha paper floating around down there about a Miss Melody Jones appearing in Some Omaha girls' club amateur theatricals—we-ell, I just had to hop on the bus, run up there, and call—and see if by some remote chance my old friend Paul Ashbrooke's quaint idea *had* evolved. And sure enough—it had! For 'Melody Jones' was Melody Ashbrooke, orphan, living with her aunt."

The girl appeared, however, for some reason, to be mentally riveted upon the matter of her father's early days. Though perhaps, too, it was because she was now in the presence of one who'd known her father "way back when," that she asked the odd question she did, "Mr. MacWhorter, did my father, in the days that you knew him, ever mention having had a woman friend named—well—Goldie?"

"A woman friend named Goldie?" he repeated. And with kindly tolerance added: "Goldie who?"

"I—I—I don't know. Just a woman friend named Goldie—that's all."

"Well, my dear," MacWhorter endeavoured to point out, "when you reflect that the name Goldie has been applied to countless millions of blonde women in show-business, as a guide to identify any certain woman it's—it's worse than nothing."

"That's just the trouble," the girl said fiercely. "As—as an identifier it's—it's just utterly useless. It's no good."

"Does the identity of a woman named Goldie, back along the line of your father's life, and who could be dead today easily enough—probably is—mean so much to you?"

"Nothing whatever," she said incisively. "Quite nothing. I wouldn't even have bothered to ask except that I sat in the presence of one who had known Father."

"Well, suppose then," he said, "that since it doesn't matter, I take advantage—fatherly advantage only, however—of the fact that you and Bill *did* have conversation, of a sort, and friendly I trust, before he went to Chicago, perhaps you'll tell me whether his business was, by any chance, the negotiating of that round-trip Strato-Clipper passage to London which he owns? Thanks to winning it from the Associated Wine Makers of America for guessing closer than anyone in the country to the annual wine yield last year. He's not negotiating that passage, by any chance, is he, for money?"

"Oh, no," the girl said, quite emphatically. "It's not negotiable, Mr. MacWhorter. It's not even transferable."

"I knew that," MacWhorter nodded, "yes—but I just thought that Bill, being an ingenious sort of a fellow, might have worked out an angle. To discount it heavily, I mean, and sell it. You see, he went off in such a hurry there at Gurney Falls that—but all right. Well, his trip isn't, by any chance, to contact that mail-order school there that is going to teach physiognomy by mail?"

"No, Mr. MacWhorter, as far as I know—well, Bill frankly told me that he intends to remain in winechemistry. After, I mean, he takes his year in the open."

"Good!" said MacWhorter, immensely relieved. "I wouldn't want to see him desert a profession for a quack trade that would only—but here!—suppose I get back to what really matters around here. Yes, this—this depression of soul that's doing things to you—really doing things to you, Melody. Is all this depression anything growing out of—well—out of the particular esteemed member of our troupe who calls himself DiValo the Illusionist, but whom I, so help me, will continue to call just—Jules?"

"No. To me, he's always been awfully nice."

"I see," MacWhorter said, "and therefore creating a triangle that shouldn't exist—in our little show. I'm hoping—you can't stop me from hoping, you know," he amended quizzically, "that the strange territory we'll shortly be heading into will do beneficial things to you. In the way of—of taking you out of yourself. So run on back now to your trailer. You can now get a fine sleep tonight, in view of the fact that we don't pull out, this time, till tomorrow. And soon—yes, by the time that Bill Chattock returns—with solutions of ragpicker murders, and other mysterious business completed—we'll be heading into that strange territory I've been telling you about."

And as the faintest flicker of a rising interest seemed to show on the girl's face—or so MacWhorter felt certain—he went on:

"Hillbilly country, my dear," he described, "of the most extreme kind. Country which has been called in some geographies 'Little Australia' because of its unbridged distances. There'll be people along the line of our show who don't even have radios. Or motion pictures. They're intellectual savages, no less. So poverty-stricken and illiterate that—that we don't even try to play along the road, even if we could find an area along it big enough for a lot, which we couldn't. But we actually *do* play—and this should interest you—in a town further on beyond called Foleysburg, where there are no phones—no electric lights—no—again a fact!—the town is peopled chiefly by members and descendants thereof, of a sect who believe Electricity is the Devil, but whether or not, the town is built upon land granted originally by the founder of the sect, a crank named Foley, who provided that no electricity could ever be brought in or on any building sites. Yes, Foleysburg will interest you no end. You're going to see sights, Melody—regions—people—customs—things that—well things you'll enjoy no end. You'll see!"

"Yes." Her tone was but polite response. "I'll go now," she added.

She rose, the magazine for Karl the Klown under her slender forearm, turned, went silently to the trailer door, opened it, and went out. And Angus MacWhorter, left alone again with his colourless ascetic furniture, his blackthorn cane and his Bible, stroked his chin in helpless futility.

"Not just melancholy or mere spiritual depression that's fallen on that girl," he said sagely. "It's tragedy that's struck. Tragedy, yes! Of the deepest kind. But of a kind that she can tell nobody. Least of all, me."

And the huge frock-coated proprietor of Macwhorter's Mammoth Motorized Shows turned back again to his Bible, to finish his now twice-interrupted daily chapter therein. And then to take his nightly walk "under the stars with God!"

CHAPTER IV

BAD NEWS FOR BILL CHATTOCK

Bill Chattock, once wine-chemist, today circus driver, but seated just now at a table in a corner of the writing-room of the London-bound trans-Atlantic Clipper, the famous 10-Hour Strato-Bullet, motioned to the middle-aged, red-haired, white-clad hostess who was arranging some writing materials on the other side of the two tables.

Bill looked, he knew, like anything else but an ocean-jumping traveller, with his purple corduroy working trousers tucked into shin-high, thong-laced yellow cowhide boots, his sun-scorched blue serge coat, and his soft-collared blue shirt with knitted grey tie, held in at the waist by the intricately-braided leather belt.

No one else was in the writing-room but Bill Chattock himself, and the hostess; indeed, most of the passengers were, at this hour of 7 in the evening "plane time," at the bar, far up ahead. The red-haired woman, no doubt once, years ago, a blooming hostess on a trans-continental airline in the early days of air travel, but today a veteran hostess of the greater skyways, stepped to his table.

"Yes, sir? And what can I do for you?"

"How many hours—8?—7?—6?—or what-have you!—will it be, do you calculate, Miss Avonsmith—Avonsmith is your name I'm told—before we find ourselves in England?"

She looked at a gold watch on her wrist.

"I'm really afraid, Mr. Chattock—and Chattock is your name, I know—I'm afraid I'm really not the proper person to give you the exact answer you undoubtedly wish. For it is a matter of astronomy and all, you know? But when I was last up in the navigator's cabin, they were taking position and making new determinations, and so"—she dropped her wrist with the watch on—"the correct place- and flying-announcement will be coming off yonder wall loud-speaker in about 7 minutes more or less." She nodded her red head back of herself toward a speaking device high up on a wall, but looking down on the two tables in the small room.

"Be it so then," Chattock acquiesced.

The woman was now leaving the enclosure, and he was quite alone. He did not, however, indulge in any "home-made" flying calculations, based upon plane clocks, none of which he had looked at anyway for some hours, or upon a watch that had, by this time, thanks to its hands still running on a schedule which was that of America's Southwest, reached a point of hopeless unreliability. Instead, he took out from his breast pocket a letter which he'd received in Chicago but an hour before flying.

It had been mailed, this particular letter, in a bright pink envelope in the corner of which, crudely printed in jet-black capitals, was but the single address THE MacWHORTER SHOWS, with two blank lines beneath for the insertion by any user of a return-address picked out from along the future route, but with none, in this case, upon it—since, indeed, its recipient knew the route better than anyone in it. Only a scribbled "Melody Ashbrooke" along the left edge showed from whom it had emanated. Its address, handwritten in ink so that, no doubt, it could not smudge in transit, contained just the simple words "Bill Chattock" with, underneath them, the further words "Showman's Hotel, Chicago." And as the man proceeded to take out the tightly-folded sheaf of thin white sheets the envelope contained, they could be seen to have been written, not in pen, but in pencil; the first one, as Bill had been able shrewdly to deduce, while a certain trailer had been in motion; the subsequent ones after that trailer had come to a stop!

And scowling blackly, Bill Chattock brought his attention to bear on this most disconcerting, most discomposing epistle which he'd read already now 6 times aboard this plane, and would no doubt read another 6 times yet. It ran:

My very, very dear one,

I have, I fear, some bad, bad news to break to you—at least bad, *if* you really do love me as much as you say you do—there in Chicago where this will reach you, or at wherever it may get forwarded to you.

For you are, of course, not a whit closer to finding a lead to the one and only thing in the entire Universe that could make possible our marriage—and, at the same time, reveal the inside facts of the so-called Ragpicker Joe killing of years back, not that that matters much in your and my scheme of things—you are no closer, Bill, to finding this one and only thing than you were when you left here. For the sad, sad reason, Bill, that the thing—just does not exist. And never—did exist! And so—

But—to that bad news. As *you* may term it. And here it is, Bill:

Not only is it still 101 per cent impossible—and must always now be, so long as life goes on for the both of us—for *me* to marry *you*—you, my dear one, of all persons in the world!—but worse—I have decided, in my own mind, to marry Jules—or DiValo, because, as now turns out to be the case, he is in a position very, very much like the one I am in.

I came to this firm and irrevocable decision—about marrying Jules, I mean—last night, Bill, in the night, after an unhappy interview with Mr. MacWhorter in which he showed plainly he was greatly disturbed at noting how crushed I've been. I wouldn't have, for the world, of course, told him the reason, since my father had been his friend. Yes, Bill, I'm going to leave the show, with Jules, at Foleysburg, which town lies up ahead of us now some 8 days yet—or 7 days from when you receive this letter. Friday the 13th!—in case you haven't the playing schedule with you. I'm going to "jump show," Bill, at close of evening's performance that night, for at that point, and at that hour, as you yourself must have heard, the show goes on into hopeless territory where there are no railroads nor anything. At Foleysburg, where the show will proceed to dive into this railroadless, flying-fieldless territory, Jules and I can still walk westward some 5 miles along a certain road—and catch a single-track jerkwater train that goes past there at 2 in the morning and stops on red-lantern signal.

So Foleysburg it is, Bill—and Friday the 13th!—where I leap off into a new life. You are asking here, perhaps, why, if I'm going to do this, I wait till Foleysburg. Ah, Bill, it's a 4-way "must," my leaving and all at Foleysburg only, and not before. A 4-way "must"! For, first of all, I shall in that way at least be giving you the full 10 days I promised to give you to run down this hopeless angle that will "remove the non-existent shadow from me" as you put it. Secondly, I shall, in that way, have lived fully up to my agreement with Mr. MacWhorter to remain with him to no less than the end of my 20th year, since Friday the 13th next—unlucky Friday the 13th!—is my birthday, you see—my 21st birthday. Thirdly, as I told you, Foleysburg is the last chance to hop to Civilization before the show goes into "no human being's land" as some of the old-timers in the show call it. And fourthly—well, now you have it, Bill—my birth registration slip, with fingerprint identification, and that passport I took out when I thought to go to France with Aunt Olivia, will establish me as being 21, and legally marryable in that state without residence, *only* after 11 P.M. of the night we play there.

And so now straight to the subject foremost in your mind. Why am I marrying a man named Jules DiValo, when, presumably, I love you?

Well, for one thing Jules loves me. For another thing, he is confident that no matter how I feel—or think I feel—about you now, today, I'll feel that way to him after being Mrs. Jules DiValo for a while. Thirdly, as I myself had to learn, alas, that night I foolishly had you open for me, and read aloud to me, Aunt Olivia's letter in the trailer—and in the presence of Jules, as well—and all because I was late in making up my face, and wanted to kill several birds with one stone. And in that letter was brought out—before you could even arrest your words—Aunt Olivia's regretful disclosure to me that Father had revealed to her, before he died, that he and Mother had never really been married. I knew in that instant, Bill, that our romance was ended. Because Aunt Olivia has always told me the truth about all things, and has—

The man reading the letter made comment, half aloud:

"A devil—that half-aunt of hers," he said, "if there's anything at all to the science of reading character from photographs. Why—with those thin lips of hers—those brooding lines between her brows—she's the type that will wait for years to strike somebody she wants to hurt. And what could have hurt Melody worse than striking that girl down in her most sensitive spot—her legitimacy—why, it's unbelievable. Not that I can do a damned thing about it, but I still can wonder why in hell Olivia Garpow, spinster, is doing this malignant thing to her own half-brother's innocent child? But having now put herself on record, in her own handwriting, in that damned letter of hers, that Paul Ashbrooke told her he'd never married Melody's mother, she's of course destroyed the marriage certificate she must have had—so that it can never show up, even after her own death."

The letter resumed, at the top of the next page:

But don't, dear Bill, write back to me and try to argue me out of my decision as you tried that night, after the show. For as I said then—and I say it again, Bill, for the last time—with *my* parents not married—and *yours* married by bell, book and candle and all the trimmings!—I'd only be a bad-luck piece for you—yes, Bill, those things work out that way; unlike set-ups just don't mix. And that is why, Bill, my fate definitely became to marry somebody exactly like myself. And this—is where Jules comes in. For after he'd heard my deplorable case from your reading of Aunt's letter—after we left Gurney Falls, in fact—he came to me and told me unhappily about *his* case. Even showed me the clipping that confirmed it. He is a so-called test-tube baby, Bill! From a famous Paris clinic. Never can he throw up to any girl that her parents were not married, and that she is a bastard. For he doesn't even *know* who his progenitors were. His mother was just a woman with amnesia, and she never did emerge from it during the brief life she had up to, and following, his birth. He virtually has no parents at all, in the ordinary sense of the word. I can never bring disgrace to him—he can never issue the slightest oblique statement against *my* birth—neither of us are in position to throw anything up to the other. But because, Bill, you are trying so hard to run this hopeless thing down, let me at least honour your effort by giving the facts, in writing, concrete as to dates, etc. I was 5 when the incident about the orange-leafed book came up. It was my birthday. Father had been home for some months— "resting," as the show-business term goes! I had asked Father that day, there in St. Louis where we then lived—had asked him, childlike, what city he and Mama had been married in. Right after he'd been showing me her picture, taken just before she died, and when of course I was but 2, and telling me her name had been just Mary Smith, and that she'd been an orphan and minus all relatives of all kinds. And he said, "Honey, you have no more chance, at 5, of remembering a town and a state than you have of repeating your Mother Goose backward. Now I'll tell you how, honey, you can always find out the town. You see that library across the way. A month ago, honey, when I was locked out here one day because I forgot my keys, and it was raining hard, I wandered in there. And took down from a shelf a little thin book. A book with orange leaves, honey—same colour exactly as the little dress you love most of all your dresses. According to a typewritten card tacked on the edge of the shelf, this little book was the only copy of itself in the entire world, not that that means anything whatsoever to you, no. But it held a poem, and lo, in one of its lines—one that papa happened to be reading over and over again, because he's an actor and he saw what a scrumptious piece of delivery that part of the poem would make for him in a stage part—well, as I read and re-read that line, honey, I thought I saw in it the town and state where your mama and I were married. And when I tried it out, sure enough—there they were—I was right! So now you've got something you can always remember. And, having seen your papa make a number of stage deliveries already in your small life, *will* remember! Little thin book?—with orange leaves? Long poem in it?—like the things in your Alice? Single speech that papa would have liked to have delivered?—in costume and all?—on a stage? Town and state held in one little teeny line of that speech?"

And right there, Bill, things happened that were to end all discussion about orange-leafed books and everything else—for many years. Aunt came in from downtown at that second. In her hand a special-delivery letter she'd taken from the messenger up the street. It was to Father. An invitation that he join a certain theatrical stock company in the East, and quickly. And, Bill, I never saw my Father again for four and one half long years. For playing first a bit part in that show, he became its lead, and finally its manager. And I thought no more about the orange-leafed book. For Father's reference to an actual paper in Aunt's possession seemed to— to sort of satisfy my young mind. I did go across the city to that library that had been across from where we had lived. And tried, in it, to see the orange-leafed book—the "thin orange-leafed book that had contained a long poem"—that Father's own hands had leafed over. But—it wasn't there, then, Bill. It was gone! For good. Oh yes, they remembered the book well. The kind lady librarian was even willing to tell a child of 11 all about it. It was called just Beowulf. Was a translation of what, as I understand it, is the earliest known piece of Anglo-Saxon literature. And the author of this translation was a highly erratic scholar named Hans Eigruber—trained in his youth as a printer. A man who differed so markedly with all other translators of Anglo-Saxon, that the few scholarly publishers who had seen his manuscript of Beowulf, had refused to even consider it for publication And so, in a typically Teutonic rage he'd set the work up in type himself on some home equipment, and had run it off, page by page, on a hand press, on orange paper. And had donated this one single copy to this museum.

But why the book was no longer there in the library-museum, Bill, I can add nothing more than what I told you that night. Namely, that the library-museum trustees had finally come to deem the book a crank book, and so had sold it, together with several other unwanted volumes, at a book-auction held in the library, where it had been purchased by an obvious Englishman; and all that he told of himself was that he had been touring America; was on his way back home. Anyway, he'd paid $25 for the book, had given no name, and had taken it away. All this the lady librarian told willingly.

Later—some months later—seeing a picture in a St. Louis paper of a shop in London called the "If-We-Can't-get-the-Book-it-Doesn't-Exist-Shop," I wrote to them. But they wrote back that they had never heard of it; had no record of ever having handled it, or even of its having been handled in the book-trade; could do nothing for me. And so that—was that!

But now, Bill, while I'm on the subject of the vanishing of that book from the general picture, I have further news yet. News that will knock even your optimism right out of your being. You see, I wired Aunt Olivia after you left, asking her for all details about the book that *she* might know of. And she sent me, together with something else, a newspaper clipping about the very purchase of the book from that museum-library across from us. 'Twas from a first page—'twas headed, with a 2-column head, LIBRARY-MUSEUM OF RARE VOLUMES SELLS ORANGE-LEAFED BEOWULF BECAUSE OF CRANK SCHOLARSHIP—I'm not enclosing it here because Jules, to whom I loaned it, lost it. But what is of significance, Bill, is that the clipping shows itself to have been a front-page story, and its date, a part of the whole clipping, shows that the sale of the book to the unknown and in-transit Englishman had been full 2 weeks *before* Father blithely told me his fantastic little tale of an orange-leafed book that contained a "poem" with a "declamatory speech" that contained a "line" that itself contained the "letters of" "his and mother's place of marriage" held within it! The use of that particular book, in his tale, *was* his "out," since the book was gone into the unknown.

I was 10½ the day that Father, home for the first time in years, took me proudly to visit an old friend in the profession who was dying. You may therefore rely fully on my memories of that day. Somehow, something came up at the bedside about this so-called Ragpicker Joe Murder that had taken place many years back—before even I was born and all—in Chicago. I owned a Negro rag doll at the time, and my small ears were very, very much attuned to such subjects as black ragpickers. So they took in everything, rest assured! Father, thinking probably but to entertain a dying man, said: "Ben, it may surprise you, but I know the whole inside facts of that strange murder. Though my lips are sealed till all the parties involved are dead. You see, I received them, in confidence, from a party called—well, Goldie—I can't very well give you the last name of course. Unfortunately, all involved are *not* dead today. The murderer, for one—"

"—and Goldie," nodded the old man. "Which *does* tie your lips. But Paul—you owe it to the Future of Crime Analysis to write those facts out, somewhere, against the day when *all* the parties are dead."

And Father said, Bill—and without cracking a smile—and there's where the Romancer came in: "That's exactly what I did, Ben. For at the time I married this child's mother, the old clergyman of the church where I'd fixed to have the ceremony done, told me that he always urged people getting married in that place to set down, on the back of the rectory marriage-book page, which they both would sign, all family facts or data that preferably should be preserved. And so, Ben, having then had the facts of that murder in my possession all of a year—with the result that they were ever so vivid—I wrote out a full account of them—complete even to all the names involved—coded it by a unique coding system I've invented—and transferred the coded transcription to the back of that page."

Thus Bill, Father's blithe tale, uttered no doubt perhaps only to pacify a dying man. And—anyway, a little later we left Ben. Father, in full blooming health, went down that night with pneumonia, and died in 48 hours. Within a few minutes, indeed, of old Ben across the city, as I afterward learned. After which Aunt Olivia moved, with me, to Omaha. And that is that!

And so now I do enclose you three items here—one sent me by Aunt Olivia today with the clipping confirming quite her revelation to me that Mother and Father were never married—the other two constituting some items that were amongst Father's personal things when he died, and dug up by me only last night amongst my own personal things, and which do at least prove that he did know the facts of that murder—though of course his recording them on the back of any marriage-book page appears quite impossible in the face of all the other circumstances.

The first is the bottom-most part of a letter from Father to Aunt Olivia, which she tore off and retained, she says, against the day she would *have* to tell me the unfortunate facts.

Here the man reading the letter detached, morosely, something held to the back of the sheet by a pin. And gazed at it sourly. It was, indeed, the bottom-most part of a page of handwriting, and it read:

and that, Olivia, is why I never married the girl's mother. For

"Pish!" the man commented audibly. "He's but referring here to some actress, in some road company, who had a daughter, and—why, the photo of the woman he did marry is the picture of a woman who would never, never live openly with a man. She'd die first."

He went on, skipping half a line.

The other two—and which I would like back eventually, since they are mementoes of my father—would like them, in fact, mailed care of my Aunt Olivia, should circumstances dictate that you and I shan't meet again—are self-explanatory. They were found amongst Father's papers, the letter having been written, as you'll note, but a week before he died—hence something more than 10 years or so ago from now.

Chattock now detached a clip at the side of the page and transferred around in front of it two items that had been merely clipped there. The frontmost was a letter—unfinished—in the same handwriting as the scrap that Olivia Ashbrooke had enclosed to her niece. It bore a date which was less than 11 years ago, and read:

Dear Goldie,

Chancing today upon a true-crime-story magazine which purports to partly "explain"—chiefly through the use of certain findings, but utterly ridiculous theories of a police-investigator named Frank DuShane!—a certain bizarre occurrence in Chicago, of some years back, which had its final culmination in the Hotel Romanorum there, I was inexorably led to write you a letter. Particularly because, Goldie, I'd found, but the day before, in one of the estimable trade journals devoted to our profesh, that you are alive and kicking. And I do so want to know how you are today, these considerable years later? I need not add, Goldie, that the facts of that occurrence, so fully confided to me by you, have never been divulged to any living person, and never will be, certainly not so long as any of the parties involved are alive.

As for the mere fact that the wielder of the dagger goes about in the world today free and unrestrained, and all that—well, this case is an intricate case, to say the least. To my mind, you are the only one to be considered. And besides, I subscribe myself to the Hindu Law of Karma, which says that every action participated in by anyone is returned to them in the exact degree of ill involved. And—but what I started out to say, Goldie, is that I do find myself still utterly amazed with respect to the manner in which the criminological investigative world quite fails to grasp, with respect to that affair, the possible relationship to it of a man dead many, many years before it took place. Yes, I refer to J. Hanborn Eliffe, Ph.D., Professor of Latin and Roman History, who built the idiotic hotel on inherited money. In some ways, it has always seemed to me that that whole affair is a brilliant mosaic, and he—dead for decades—his ashes even resting, if one reference in one story is correct, in a Roman-like urn in Rosehill Cemetery, Chicago!—he is the missing piece of the mosaic that gives it intelligibility. And that—but enough of all this, Goldie. I—

Here the letter came to a stop. Either its writer had never got around to resuming it, because of his own death—or had come to the conclusion it were best not sent in the mails. Which, would never be known.

Transferring this item to his breast pocket, Bill Chattock now proceeded to examine the other item which had been clipped with it to the back of the sheet. And which was nothing more than two extremely thin cardboard circles. Lettered crudely on the centre of the foremost one was

THE CODOSCOPE—PATENT TO BE APPLIED
FOR BY PAUL ASHBROOKE

and Bill recognized it immediately as presenting a principle of coding not even patentable: namely, the use of a scrambled—or code—alphabet which could be placed in any of 26 positions with respect to the true alphabet it represented. With a sigh, he transferred this, too, to his breast pocket, and took up the last page of Melody Ashbrooke's letter.

> But of what earthly use, Bill, is the fact that Father might have known, or even did know, the solution of a murder to write out on the back of a church-rectory marriage-registry book page—and even had a coding system in which to code it—when there could be no such rectory marriage-registry page? For the simple reason that—there had been no marriage?
>
> So now you know all the fine details—have everything—not omitting the fact that I am going to marry Jules DiValo. And for the sad but simple reason that he is one human being in the world who can never sit across the breakfast table from me and call me—or even think of me—as illegitimate. However, Bill, as I also said, it won't and can't be before Foleysburg. And the 13th, or evening thereof. So-o-o—with your penchant, as you've described it to me so often, of always giving birthday presents that aren't material, you have all the time in the world yet, you see, to come and lay in my lap, on that fateful 13th, that little birthday present I know you'd like most in the entire world to give *me*—yes, the proof that Father and Mother were married.
>
> But I know too, Bill, that if you fail to get anywhere in this mad chase, you'll just see to it that you don't rejoin the show till I'm out of it.
>
> Better just forget me, Bill. And forget even that I said, not long ago, that you I loved best. Forget me, please. It's all so hopeless—don't you see?
>
> Melody.

And now, having reached the end of the long letter, Bill Chattock sat for a moment, and at the end of that moment, he tore the combined sheets clear across, then across again at right angles, and finer and finer, finally transferring the fragments to his side coat pocket for strewing away at such time and place where they could never be put together again.

And to himself he spoke again, and as bitterly as before.

"She's quite and utterly sold by the damning fact that her dear Auntie never hurt her before—or lied to her before. Of course not! Olivia Garpow's brooding face shows she's the type to make it stick—*when* she does do it! Lord knows what does activate the Garpow woman. Who—but what does it matter, anyway? For there's no chance to budge this particular obstacle.

But one thing *is* certain: If what that unknown Englishman, who bought that orange-leafed Beowulf years ago, said that day to the St. Louis reporters is true—that it possesses *some* flashes of 'interpretive genius'—then it's not destroyed, wherever it's wandered to, during the years, over there in England. If—if only because it carries a notice in itself that it's the only copy of itself. And *if* what that Englishman there in Chicago tells me is true, then the book—if it exists in England—should be findable through this man in London, this man at 17 Brunswick Square known as 'Old 1-2-3'—"

"Attention—everybody aboard the Clipper-plane 10-Hour Strato-Bullet," came off the loud-speaker in the wall above Bill's head. "We are happy to announce, here in the navigation cabin, that this plane will be landing at Clipper Basin, Lower Thames, in about a half-hour. In short, friends and voyagers on this uneventful, but we trust interesting, trip—London, England—in 30 minutes!"

CHAPTER V

EPISODE IN LONDONTOWN

Mr. Penruddock Gill, of 17 Brunswick Square, London, made another of his moves on his great chessboard on which he was working out tonight's daily chess problem as presented in the *London Evening Ledger.* And it was right here that the door-bell of the great house in Brunswick Square sounded. Mr. Gill rose creakingly to answer it, for he had no servants today, a charwoman coming in every morning to do the small amount of work necessary. He went out of the library, and down the high-ceilinged damask-papered hall, and opened the great door, a thing which, with his 77 years, took considerable effort.

The open door revealed a man of about 26 or 28—at least so far as Mr. Gill could judge—with a small light-coloured air-travel-overnight bag in his hand. The caller wore very odd habiliments, however; certainly so, so far as one might see around and about London. For on his head was a broad-brimmed, grey-felt, Stetson-like hat, and on his feet were shin-high, thong-laced, yellow cowhide boots into which were laced—purple corduroy trousers! The braided belt that peeped from between the open blue serge coat, with its bare suggestion of too-short sleeves, and that held in a soft-collared but impeccably clean blue shirt with neat knitted grey tie, was a weird thing of many braidments.

"Good evening," the old man managed to say. His eyes fell back again to the bag. "If it's Dyerly House, which takes lodgers, that you seek, that would be at the exact diagonally opposite corner of the—"

"But it isn't," said the caller. "It's—but does Mr. Penruddock—Gill live here?"

"He does," said the old man. Then added experimentally: "Is now speaking."

"Oh—fine. Oh, boy. Whoops! I was hoping against hope that Fate wasn't going to tweak my—but my name is Chattock. William T. Chattock. Of—well, of Wine City, U.S.A., so far as my last permanent address went. Or of Chicago—so far as my last place of residence went. I've just flown straight here. From Chicago, to get information which—well, Mr.

Gill, it's information I need badly, sorely, and which perhaps only you in the entire world can give me. A Mr. Isherwood of Hammersmith—wherever that might be—gave me your name and address, in Chicago, where he was acting as exchange professor at the University of Chicago. But I'd learned of your existence—and the fact that his old friend Professor Isherwood in Chicago would give me your actual name—from a Mr. Dardwin Kettlewell, of Harrow—wherever *that* too might be!—in a small town called Gurney Falls. A small town where I happened to be, at the moment I came head on with a very distressing and baffling problem. Mr. Kettlewell was a lawyer—solicitor I think you call such over here?—or is it barrister?—anyway, he gave me the facts of your existence and the furthermore facts which seemed to indicate that you only could possess the exact information I need."

"Well, well, well," was all Mr. Gill could say. Adding, "'Pon my word—this is the first time anybody ever literally stepped right across a thousand miles of land and one ocean—to consult—Kettlewell did you say? Dardwin Kettlewell?" He stood hastily aside from the cramped opening he had been maintaining. "I'm so deucedly disconcerted, don't you know, at meeting up in person with the possessor of the original 7-League Boots, that—won't you step in, sir?"

The American lost no time in getting inside, where Mr. Gill, closing the door gently, nodded down the hallway to that one open portal through which poured plentifully generous light. "My chess-problem room," he said dryly. "Would you repair in there, please?"

The American promptly led the way thither, but did step aside when Mr. Gill came up in his rear, and humbly followed his host inside. Mr. Gill drew over a Queen Anne blue-velvet upholstered chair to face the armchair in which he had previously been sitting, but turned the latter 90 degrees around, and away from the chessboard. "If you'll take either chair," he invited courteously.

The American took the one he was supposed, under the laws of Youth meeting up with Age, to take. The uncomfortable one! The Queen Anne chair. Mr. Gill lowered himself into his armchair.

"Might I ask," he said quizzically, "why, if I *do* have information you need, you—ah—came here in person? In view, I mean, of the existence of the Atlantic cable—and long-distance telephone service—and—"

"You may indeed," returned the American promptly. "It is because I would almost certainly have to follow up whatever I may get from you, here in England. And if I don't get from you what I must have—then it's still here in England that I'll have to try the next thing. Which as yet I have no idea what it may be. That's the reason."

"Yes, I see," nodded Mr. Gill. "You must be frightfully intent on gaining your objective, Mr. Chattock—Chattock was the name, was it not?—for the expense of coming here by air—it seems to me you even spoke, sir, of not having too much of the world's goods, and—Now the fare on that 10-Hour Strato-Bullet is, I understand—you really mean you flew here by that plane?—to consult with me?"

"Well, if 'twasn't the Strato-Bullet I came on, Mr. Gill, then the Great Circle Airways sure took my passage under false pretences! I am a circus driver. But only due to a matter of health that started to fail some time back, and the kindness of an old friend—the man who owns the little circus—of my father's who happened to note my whiteness of complexion, and insisted on putting me out into the open for a year. But my actual profession is chemist. Rather, wine-chemist. So it's not altogether so surprising that about a year ago I should have won a lottery-like affair held by the Associated Wine Growers of America, involving guessing the annual wine yield for that year in the U.S.A. in gallons—yes, I guessed it, and won the 3rd prize. Which was a paid-up, non-transferable round-trip passage from Chicago to London. And that's the story of how one featherless chick flew right over the barnyard fence and landed in the next county! But it happens furthermore—not that it makes any difference to yours truly—that my solving the problem which I hope like the devil to solve through you, will mean also incidentally that I'll have the solution of a certain old murder that happened a quarter-century ago in Chicago. A murder quite inexplicable from the viewpoint of motive and everything."

"Good—heavens!" Mr. Gill ejaculated helplessly. "I am quite hopelessly bewildered."

"I don't blame you for so being, Mr. Gill," laughed the American. "And now that the amenities around here are consummated I'll proceed to lay on the line exactly what I have to know. Which, if I get it, will promptly send me winging my way back to America in less than 24 hours. But here goes. And Lawd, oh Lawd, he'p dis po' niggah—he'p him now!"

Mr. Gill passed a helpless wrinkled hand over his forehead at this buoyant infant who ushered in his request with a fervent Negro prayer, but bent, all attention.

"Well, Mr. Gill," began the American, "to introduce the subject, this British barrister, Mr. Kettlewell, told me that there was one person in all England who probably knew today the exact location of all books in England which exist in but a sparse number of copies. Or so, anyway, he said he'd heard once, from a friend of his who seemed to know much about the individual in question. He gave me your actual name and address here in London, and told me, specifically, that you knew the location of all books in England that exist in but 1, 2, or 3 copies. He—he said that it was your hobby to enter methodically, on large filing cards, the names and addresses of the last-known owners of such books; and all new data that came up on such books; and he even said you were known here as Old 1—ah—er—skip it, please."

The old man, knowing quite well he was known in the British book trade as Old 1-2-3, smiled tolerantly.

"And so," Chattock said, "in the face of all this, Mr. Gill, can you tell me anything at all of the location in England today of an orange-leafed book— that is, printed on orange paper, that definitely came over to this country about 16 years or so ago, in the hands of some native thereof, though the book itself was actually published in the United States. Self-published, that is—in a one-copy edition. To make it—well—rare. And donated to a muse-um-library. And—but the name of it is Beowulf—though it's a most erratic translation of that poem by a—"

"—a German named Eigruber?" took up the old man gently. "Hans— Eigruber?"

He stopped. Arrested by the manner in which his odd caller sat up, face radiant. "Glo—ree hallelujah, Mr. Gill," the latter said.

"You know of the book! You—"

"Yes," said Mr. Gill. "I know of the book. Through the simple fact that the man who purchased it in America brought it to me years ago for an opinion as to what value it might have. And—oh, no—this man isn't alive today—I may even tell you that his small library of books were sold by his executors to some dealer in our East End—most were of really no value whatever—they obviously became 'bin books'—for the particular book you describe wound up in an open bin in front of a shop in the Whitechapel High Road—priced at sixpence! 12 cents, young man, in your money. And—well you see I *do* know something about the travels, in and about England any-way, of books in 1 copy only. And I have the facts about this particular book fresh in mind, moreover," Mr. Gill explicated painstakingly, "thanks to hav-ing had a phone-call about it only 2 months ago—and getting out my card on it. Yes, the book was picked up in that bin on Whitechapel High Road by—"

He stopped, thoughtfully.

"—by a man," he said, a bit cryptically, "who is himself dead today. And whose estate—which was considerable—is tied up today in a sort of trust. For it's being held for the benefit of his only surviving relative. A daughter. Who—yes, she lives in England, though not in London. She is un-married—not that that has anything to do with it, has it?—and she—but you want her name, don't you, Mr. Chattock? So you can charter a 6-motored air-liner, and rush there."

"Yes, Mr. Gill. Not that I'll charter any plane, no—though I'll probably get me a seat on the very first one that goes there—wherever 'tis—yes, I do want it. And how I—"

"And that's just it," said Mr. Gill firmly. "Mr. Chattock from the U.S.A., I can hardly take on myself the responsibility of sending a strange man hurtling to a lone woman's home to see about a book which—a man—a man who—"

"—who looks like a movie bad-man out of a B-picture?" nodded Chattock, looking down at himself, and quite critically. "Yes, I quite get the allusion. I might, for all you know, pull a six-shooter out of my hip pocket and hold this woman up? Or—or—"

"We-ell," said Mr. Gill, "I hardly think you'd do that. Still, this *is* England, you know. Where—well I can't be responsible for bringing together strangers. At least one a stranger to me."

"I get you, Mr. Gill. In short, you feel you've a right to know why I must have this Beowulf book in my hands; whether it's a criminal matter, or not. Isn't that correct?"

"We-ell," said Mr. Gill helplessly, "I don't like to say it. But—but that's the way it is. This is England, you know! And in bringing together two people—as a pure intermediary—I am responsibl—well, I have to use discretion."

"I understand," said Chattock. "Well, here are the facts, Mr. Gill. The facts devolving about a girl who had an actor for a father—a girl who is confident today that she's a—"

And he proceeded, ever so logically and concisely, to set forth a curious set of circumstances. The facts themselves centered about a girl—the narrator called her simply Simone—Mr. Gill was quite confident that the American was protecting her identity, and that was all right with him—a girl who was a "spot girl" in a little circus called Mr. Horthy's Travelling Circus—again Mr. Gill felt confident that the identity of the circus was being held back, and he saw no objections to that. And when the story came to an end, full 10 minutes later, Mr. Gill could but shake his silvered head.

"The book which you seek," he began with no preliminaries, "was—up to two months ago—in the hands and custody of a young woman named Arvilla Eigruber—of Liverpool. German so far as her blood goes, yes—but not German by nationality. For she's English-born. No relation, Miss Eigruber, to the author of that book. But that, so she told me personally, was how her father happened to take it home from that bin on Whitechapel High Road. He was wandering about the East End of London here and came on the book in the bin. Thought it was almost certainly by a particularly scholarly relative of his, and took the book home. Well, the book just stayed on then in Gunther Eigruber's library. He died about two years ago. Leaving a considerable fortune. I made some inquiries about Miss Eigruber—as to whether she even existed! Yes, she was—Eigruber's only daughter. An heiress, yes, to the fortune which he left, though it's tied up in some small minor way of which I know nothing. Well, to conclude with Miss Arvilla Eigruber, she lives in a small but fine old Stuart residence facing Lester Gardens in Liverpool. On Furness Street. Number 17. And recently—Miss Eigruber told me all this herself—a gentle little old lady from America called there. She had been, it seems, in Europe with a party of Cook tourists—was now *en route* home via Liverpool. She called with the specific request to see that house. Miss Eigruber took her through, and the little old lady, in looking over the books on one wall, saw the Beowulf, and wanted to buy it."

"And that was why the girl called you up, eh?" said Chattock. "To see how much she should nick her for?"

"No," said Mr. Gill, "she called to find how little she could morally charge—and yet be correctly fair with respect to her father's estate, to which it seems she is accountable. I told Miss Eigruber the value was no more than 2 guineas, and probably never would be greater. Pointing out that it had an artificial rarity, and was known to have it in the book trade. So she charged the old lady 2 guineas—and the old lady took the book pridefully and proprietarily back to America with her. And that's the story, Mr. Chattock, as far as *I* can carry it. For I did not seek to elicit from Miss Eigruber the name of the next owner-to-be in America."

"But you've sure taken the story far enough to help *me* on *my* way. I've the name and address of the girl who had the book."

A silence fell, in which it could be seen that woolly worms were creeping all over the American. He looked at a silver watch, and Mr. Gill smiled at the way Americans wanted to fly about like arrows.

"You want to go at once," he said mildly, "to Liverpool. I do advise you, however, to at least wait till—sun-up."

The American had taken advantage of Mr. Gill's appraisal of his desire for speed, by instantly rising. "Oh," he said, "I won't do you wrong by trying to get Miss Eigruber to the front door in her lace-trimmed nightie. I'll try—yes—to get to Liverpool tonight—even if it's the last plane out. But I'll lay up there till the sun tries to show his chin through your English fog. And believe you me, I'll be at the door of 17 Furness Street mighty, mighty soon after Miss Eigruber has wiggled herself out of that nightie. And after that—well, Mr. Gill, I'll be winging my way back to America on the 10-Hour Strato-Rocket by tomorrow P.M. If so, I'll not have time to see you again. So—will you accept a million thanks—and my apologies for taking it this way on the heel-and-toe?"

Mr. Gill winced, and took the hand. "Don't apologize for anything," he said. "This has been a most colourful experience in the life of a lonely old man."

The American reached quickly down and took up his tiny piece of travelling luggage. And the old man, taking the hint, went on ahead of him, and conducted him to the front door. Saw him sadly down the single low front step, and out to the lamplighted sidewalk.

"Good night, sir," Mr. Gill said. "And—and oodles—isn't that the word?—oodles of luck to you."

Gently he closed the door, and went back to his chess-problem room. Stood looking down at his great chessboard, the moves on which had been so interrupted by the visit just concluded. Went to sit down and resume his problem, but instead shook his head.

"No," he said, with a sigh. "Of a sudden, somehow, this comparatively simple chess stuff—is no longer of interest. At least—not tonight. Not in the face of the kind of wild chess that young man of the cinema garb is obviously playing. For he is up against many, many moves yet—before he can get the particular chess-piece called—called Chattock!—into its proper square in its proper row. He's got to fight his way yet through all the stages—to make it come out Happiness for Two. Yes, Happiness."

CHAPTER VI

EPISODE IN LIVERPOOL

Arvilla Eigruber, dismounting in front of 17 Furness Street, Liverpool, from her taxicab, and still in her olive-green hiking costume, even to the knapsack on her shoulders, and wooden staff in hand, noted that Kurt, the old serving-man, had been in the process this morning of polishing the knocker of the door which looked out over fashionable Lester Gardens across the way. Arvilla, aged 24, a bit chunky in build despite her expensive Bond-Street-made many-suspendered and multi-belted and multi-pocketed hiking costume, none too short in height, but with china-blue Teuton eyes and taffy-coloured hair under her trig cap, and Kurt, with his close-cropped, flat-backed, block-hewn head bristling at the front with a grey stiff pompadour, were the last of the former Eigruber domicile.

"Well, Kurt," she asked, "is there anything of interest? Nothing, I suppose?"

"Nodding," said Kurt stolidly, "but dot *verdammte Amerikanner*—oxcoos it, Miss Arvilla—de Amerr-i-can again."

"The—the American?" said Arvilla, her pulse quickening a bit. "What American, Kurt? What do you mean?"

"Der vun insite dere," bit out Kurt, gesturing houseward with his polishing cloth. "Der cowpoy."

"Cowboy?" Arvilla, highly attuned to cinema westerns—indeed, she had never missed one in her life!—was all attention. "Where is this American, and what do you mean, Kurt—cowboy?"

"Hees' in der cart-room *bei*, " said Kurt. And now lowered his voice. "Com' he *hier*, Arvilla, dree day ago. Straid from Lonton. He iss on der drail of a pook—der pook what your Papa dit buy in Lonton down in Viteschapel—"

"The Beowulf? Which I sold to the little lady from—go ahead?"

"Yah, der Bey-o-vulf. He iss on ids drail. Vy, I don'd know; know I only dot he iss blenty hot unt boddered apout it. I dell him you vass on hiking drip *bei*—unt dot noputty know vere in England you are, but you *haf* to be back by der morning of der 10th of Chune, becoz of bapers to sign mid-d your zolicitors, unt vill *hier* be apout 10. But—you dink dot American iss villing to sid-d down unt be batient?"

"I—I don't know what to think," complained Arvilla. "What did *he* do?"

"Ach! Comes he *hier*—in der cart-room he sid-d-d's. For all uf 2 hours. Lest—like a vooman—dot's der vay he boots it, Arvilla, der *schwein-hund!*—lest like a vooman you get dired, *bei* hiking, uf, unt come onexpectedly home."

"A man after my own heart," said Arvilla truthfully. "One who keeps his nose on the job. Go ahead, Kurt?"

"Dot's all der iss," announced Kurt. "Diss iss der day I sait you voot come home. Unt come home you ditt—right on der dot. Unt he iss in dere—propaply valking feetbrints out uf der carpet. So moch does he pace oop unt down—oop unt down—"

"Life and death, eh," said Arvilla thoughtfully, "Well, I'll proceed in and see what this is all about."

She withdrew her silver-plated key as Kurt moved, froglike, out of the way, opened the door, and entered the heavily green-carpeted hallway. She went down the hallway with its walnut-panelled walls, past the unusually narrow carpeted staircase that rose in completely reversed direction to that of most houses, and threw open the door of the so-called card-room. And there he was, at the furthest side of the room, waiting with evident intentness. The Cowboy!

For that was how Arvilla figured him. A romantic figure that could have been of the cinema itself! He wore corduroy trousers that only technicolor would have properly showed, for they were purple—and turned into shin-high, thong-laced, yellow cowhide boots. A typical studio-property was the wide and intricately braided leather belt that held his trousers to his clean soft blue shirt. He was about 28, and sun-browned from doubtlessly chasing countless cows over the Pampas, or wherever such browsed, and by contrast the blue eyes that looked forth from his face were as cerulean as Arvilla's own.

She smiled warmly as she said:

"*Gut*—good morning. Pardon my starting to speak in German! This was my Father's pet room—and whenever I'm in it, I have a tendency to unconsciously use—but I am Arvilla Eigruber. I understand you have been—ah—very assiduous in trying to see me?"

"Good morning yourself, Miss Eigruber," the stranger said. He came briskly forward, and thrust out a sunbrowned paw. "In America, we—"

"—you shake hands, eh?" she said. "Good. I'll shake hands too. After all, this is no London drawing-room!"

It was some seconds before she withdrew her hand; it felt nice to have it held in that bearish clasp. But, propriety calling, she did withdraw it. "Won't you be seated?" she invited. "Yes, across the table there from me. And I'll take this."

He rounded the table, drew out the chair there, and sat down in it. Arvilla took the chair across from him, where she could glance up above his head and view her father's face—perhaps be guided by occultly-radiated messages from him. She shoved her taffy-coloured hair out of her eyes, and surveyed her caller, still quite and utterly fascinated.

"Miss Eigruber," the man began, "my name is Chattock. William T. Chattock—"

"Bill Chattock!" she said gaily. "To everyone, I'll wager? Including"—her gayness subsided—"specially—your wife?"

"Well, I guess you've kind of called the turn on that, miss," he laughed. "Oh, I mean the handle—not the wife. For wife have I none. Yes, always was a Bill. Always will be, therefore. For—anyway, I'm a—"

"A cowboy," she put in eagerly. "From the trackless plains."

He looked down at himself. "Well, miss, not exactly. I'm—" He looked down at himself again, and a bit more speculatively. "I'm a circus-driver."

"Circus—driver!" she cried delightedly. "You mean—a travelling show—that has lions and tigers—you drive a tiger—"

"Have, miss," he said. "Off and on. Have driven every car in the outfit."

"Well, what on earth—what on earth—are you doing here in England?"

His face grew grave. "Miss Eigruber, for reasons I don't want to go into, I am seeking the name of the American lady to whom you sold the copy of Beowulf your father had. You see, I've contacted Old Mr. 1-2-3—"

"Old Mr. Gill, of London," she nodded. "I never met him. But I made inquiries of him, however—at the time the American lady wanted to buy the book."

"Well, that's just it. Miss Eigruber, I've got to see that book. I don't want it. To own, that is. I just need to be with it a few hours. I need to—to examine it, see? Line by line. Paragraph by paragraph—word by—" He stopped uneasily.

"Some old prospector," she nodded, "has coded into it—by dots or something—the location of a valuable gold-claim he's found—in the mountains. A fabulously rich claim, maybe. Dying, probably, in some lonely log cabin far from—he told you about this?"

"Well, miss," the man said cryptically, "one guess might be as good as another."

"Oh, that's it, all right," she said confidently. "That's the only thing that could catapult a man here to Liverpool in his very work clothing. Well, well, well! To think that all the two years after Father went I—I was harbouring the location of fabulous wealth."

"If you'd known it," he asked curiously, "would you have been interested? Known it, I mean, *and* the secret of its coding?"

"Heavens, no!" she said emphatically. "I like it very much in Liverpool here. I certainly wouldn't like to travel about some forsaken and deserted region with burros, and chop all day with a big pick. And dodge hostile, scalping Indians to boot! Besides, my papa did leave me a fortune. What would I want—with more than I can spend?"

"That's a satisfying philosophy, Miss Eigruber. The soundest and finest I've ever heard. Well, Miss Eigruber, how about it? I'm not asking much, am I? But what it is, it is. I've been here every day since Sunday morning. I—"

"Yes, Kurt has told me," she informed him. She looked at him pensively, even putting her elbow on the table so she could cup her chin in her hand and so attain steady unremitting vision. "Mister Bill Chattock," she said, "you may never get to that claim! It may—probably will—fizzle out. Oh, yes. For I did study geology in the course of my education—and most so-called 'claims' are nothing but out-croppings of broken-off strata which—you have nothing but the old prospector's belief. Besides, his brains may—probably were—hardened from drinking too much firewater in his day. And he may have imagined everything he told you. You maybe will find, before you are done with all this, that you have spent your life-savings, got from driving tigers and lions about the country, and hammering in tent-stakes—and got quite nowhere!"

"Right," he admitted gravely. "I might."

"You want to re-locate and stake out this nice claim," Arvilla very pointedly went on, "for what? To attain luxury. To be able to go to the theatre. To dine in *de luxe* cafes. To wear costly clothing instead of—corduroy pants. To sleep in beds that have sheets. Is this not so?"

"Well," he laughed, dryly amused, obviously, "what you set forth is logic, all right. You can't eat gold. You can't wear it. You can only exchange it for a style of life you haven't got. And since my style *is* something along the line of—of sheets in my bed—and such concomitants—I suppose you might be said to have once again called the turn on me."

"Yes," she said satisfiedly, "and I'll tell you even more, Bill Chattock. And it's that I like you. You're the first cowboy I ever knew off the screen. Oh, yes, I know—you're not a cowboy—but a circus-driver is about the same thing as a cowboy. You're good-looking. You're assiduous—in what you do. How you ever got here, I can't imag—I suppose you smuggled yourself over in the lifeboat of a liner—or came over on a cattleboat—but you got here all right, all right. For here you are. In my house! In my papa's—no—*my* card-room. And—Bill Chattock—are your ears open?"

"Wide," he said. "As two soup-plates—with no soup in 'em."

"Bill Chattock," she went on, "my papa didn't think it good that a girl remain unmarried. A girl, that is, who had never had sisters and brothers. Now me, I don't feel that way. I like to hike, and whatnot. But my papa he made my full ownership of his estate to come to me only when I have married. And provided that I enjoy a more and more limited use of it each year that married I am not. See how frank I am? Bill Chattock, listen to me now, please—Bill Chattock, you do the marrying of me that I legally require—and on the day you do it—5 minutes after the ceremony!—I'll give you the name of the woman in America who has the book. And to whom you can write—if you still then want to. Oh, I'll furnish you with the money to buy it back at any price—if now you're broke. You can even do with the book as you please. If you insist then on following it up, I will go over with you to that awful America. I'll buy a whole flock of burros. And—and gold-plated picks. I'll even sweat with you in the mountains till you find that that foolish claim is just the usual—mirage. I—"

"Oh-oh!" said the man painedly. He scratched his chin.

"Am I so awfully homely?" asked Arvilla. "Am I totally without—yes, I'll be frank—sex-appeal?"

"Good Lord, no!" he said, ever so emphatically, "You're a puh-lenty pretty gal. And you've got what it takes—of the—the other thing. Only—only—"

"Only," she demanded, though a bit nonplussed, "there is some other girl over there you have—had, that is—your eyes on? Like?"

"We-ell—yes."

"Some—some sweaty-faced girl cook in some ranch-house, of course," she declared scornfully. "Sorry! Some ranch-house girl cook was all I should have said. For—still, you aren't a cowboy at that. You're a circus-driver. All right. Some gipsy fortune-teller in your circus, then. Bill, I can make you so damned happy here in Liverpool. And of course London, too, if you like that city. I know all kinds of the nicest Cher—German peo—" She stopped. This was no bait, she saw. "I take you to theatres and night clubs—we be just with ourselves—no outsiders. We—we could burn up these two towns."

He sat back in his chair, plainly an unhappy man.

"Miss Eigruber," he began, "I—"

"Arvilla—at least?" she pleaded. "Do we have to go through a social season just to—"

"Arvilla, yes," he acceded. "Arvilla, there's more to all this than you have supposed. To get that book clears away—promises to, only, let me be honest—an obstacle in my marrying this girl. Which leaves the affair distinctly an issue, then, as between marrying her—with nothing—and marrying you—who has everything—can give me everything, we'll put it! Yes. I—I— I—Miss Eigr—Arvilla—are you a gambler?"

"I adore games of chance," she conceded frankly. "I have even studied the Laws of Probability."

"Good," he said. "I'll tell you what I'll do. I'm making *you* a proposition. The American kind. Have you a deck of cards?"

"Oh, yes, several. In the drawer here on my side of the table. Yes? Go ahead."

"Well, yank us out a deck. And I'll cut you—so help me Hannah, I will!—on the whole proposition. Makes even you gasp a bit, eh? But that's what I said! I'll cut you. Highest card—if you get it—means I'll marry you—by bell, book, and Liverpool candles—and take the info I want after the ceremony. Highest card—if I get it—means you give me that info now—free from all strings—and we'll forget about this marriage—marriage of convenience," he quickly amended.

She wondered if she looked as thoughtful as she felt. She was running over the angles of this disconcerting proposition. "You'll play ball—that's from one of your American films I last saw—you'll play ball on the arrangement because—because you'd have to. But how do you know I—is that the best you'll do?"

"Absolutely!" he said incisively. "And if it's no dice with you—on this fair, square, 50-50 chance—I'll follow my game along—along another angle."

She wondered just how much he was bluffing.

"It's a deal," she said. "It's not only better than nothing—but I'm lucky at all games that involve cards—unlucky at those that involve dice—and neither one nor the other at those involving—spinning discs!"

She drew partly open the drawer just in front of her. From the boxes of poker chips and all, including half a dozen decks of cards, she withdrew a single deck.

"Shuffle them well!" she said, and closing the drawer, shoved them across the table to him.

"Shuffle them?" he echoed. "Say—I'll do worse than that with these babies. I'll—I'll make them jig their own spots off—one ag'in the other!"

He withdrew them from their blue cardboard case. They were slender, beautiful cards—the best. He turned them over and riffled them out a ways, faces upward. Saw—as Arvilla realized, since she herself had been the last to use them—that they had last been employed in a game of solitaire. Saw this, as was quite evident, by the many suits that lay in sequence—a careless manner in which Arvilla inevitably ended a solitaire game. He looked up.

"Before we shuffle and cut—cut and shuffle," he asked, "hows-about our having one single small drink? After all, with our lives at stake—"

"Don't say that!" she corrected him. "You hurt me. Just our happiness at stake, not our lives, But you said it! About the little drink, I mean. Wait!"

She rose and crossed the room, letting herself out and closing the door gently on her prize. Crossing the narrow bit of rearway carpeted hall, she went into a small pantry, dark because of its one beautifully leaded window having been painted jet-black, and pulling on a ceiling light by means of a hanging cord, brought to view a mixing-board with a white enamelled cabinet above it.

Opening the cabinet door half-way, and exposing thereby bottles of various types on most of its shelves, her hand wavered undecidedly between the two endmost ones on the particular shelf that was level with her blue eyes. But when she finally withdrew the particular one of the bottles that she chose, the one of the two left behind was labelled Rhein Wein, while the one in her hand was a short, squat, bulbous bottle radiating great age and greater value.

Now she took from some glassware stacked along the bottom of the cabinet two delicate but minute glasses which had no companions, and, setting them down on the mixing-board, she poured into them carefully the liquor from the bulbous bottle till they stood nearly full. Now, setting the bottle off, not yet corked, she wet her fingertips, and withdrew, in succession, from the topmost shelf of the cabinet, two paper discs several inches wide on whose edges were printed, in Teutonic black letters, GESUND-HEIT. Now she dipped her index finger quite shamelessly in the liquor in the little glass marked VATER, remarking to herself as she did so, "Some of me *might* get into his blood at that, like the gipsies say." And lifting the VATER glass, she rubbed her liquor-wet finger over its entire base, then brought it down firmly on one of the paper discs. Where, of course, it stuck tightly.

Now she did the identically same operation she'd just completed with the other glass—except that she dipped her finger again into the same container. *His!*

Now, licking off her entire finger carefully so as not to waste a drop of good liquor, she poured enough more from the uncorked bottle into the despoiled glass—his!—to bring its contents not just rim-high, but bulging over the very rim. And then did the same thing with her own.

"I have now protected Papa's table," she said, "in case I can't do it. But I think I can. I will show him the steadiest hand he's ever, seen in *hi*s life."

With which, she took up the two glasses and without trying to pull out the overhanging light, transported them with such sureness and certitude that not a drop rolled over the rims of either. Her most expert work was done at the door of the room she'd originally left, For, lowering her two hands in unison and pressing the insides of them firmly against the knob, she turned it gently by raising one hand slightly—lowering the other equally so—opening the door, after the lock had clicked, with her toe—came in, and closed it behind her adroitly with a kick of her heel. Swept across the floor where the man sat, arms folded. Set the glasses down, one in front of him, one in front of her place. Not only that, but the MUTTER on hers was even turned directly to him, and the VATER on his turned to him—likewise!

"Napoleon brandy," she said nonchalantly. "How old and how expensive even I can't guess."

He appeared quite unimpressed by the name of the liquor in the glass, but was staring at the contents standing above the rim of his glass.

"Jumping—jehoshaphat, girl!" he said. "You should have been a gun-girl in the olden, golden West. What a hand! Nary a tremble in a carload."

He shook his head again in wonderment. Admiring wonderment, she felt, as she circled the table to regain her chair. But now he brought his attention back in front of himself, to the cards themselves, glumly, gloomily, a man who plainly regretted, with all his soul, ever having gone into all this.

She had now dropped back into her own place. "One question," he said, "before I shuffle the very pips off these pasteboards—one question. In case of a tie-cut, Arvilla—are you prepared to accept the old mining-camps arrangement where diamonds are high, hearts next, clubs next—and spades the least?"

"Very glad to," she acceded promptly. "I can't say I ever saw *that* brought out in the cinema—but I'll play it that way. After all, our chances are equal on anything we agree on mutually in advance. Agreed, then." Methodically, she took out the stub of a pencil from one of her many pockets, and wrote carefully out on the rim of paper protruding from under her glass. "Diamonds first, then hearts, then clubs, then spades. Right?"

"Right!" he affirmed. Now he reached forward and raised his glass, disc of paper tightly adhering. She followed suit.

"Here's to us," was all he said. "And if I lose, Arvilla, I will make you the right kind of a husband. But I warn you, if *you* lose—"

"Don't worry," said Arvilla.

"*Gesundheit!*" he offered.

"The same," she said, deeply relieved, in some vague way.

And they drank.

Now they lowered their glasses, and shoved them off, each of them, to one side. He took up the cards, and proceeded to shuffle them, ever so energetically. She fascinatedly watched the flash of the pips due to the way he partially angled the half-decks toward her—the stretches of flame from the court cards interspersed between them—like a girl in a weird dream. It—it didn't seem possible. This was *it*! The Cinema—in real life. And this hunk of man as a prize.

Now, done shuffling, he shoved the deck across the short open space between them, to her.

"Ladies first," he said. "As a gentleman, I wish you a good cut—but as a player—well, I don't!"

She shrugged her shoulders daintily. And ran her fingers gently, experimentally, down the sides of the carefully stacked and waiting deck. Felt gingerly with them to where a card protruded by a microscopic bit of itself. Not enough, to be sure, for a limping mosquito to rest a momentary foot upon, but enough to—"As good a place as any," she said to herself. "If not bett—" With which she cut, and held up the near half-deck she'd removed, at an angle where she, too, could see its face.

"Ow!" he cried, springing half-way up in his chair. He fell back. "The King—of Diamonds? Oh boy, oh boy, oh boy, oh boy, ahwoo, ah woo!"

"If you know the Laws of Probability," she said triumphantly, "you know you may as well quit now. Why not—"

"Oh, yes, I know," he responded, distress in his voice. "I know. Know that it looks already as though I'm due to be called William Eigruber. However, Chance is a most curious thing. Chance—"

He half shook his head at her.

"I mean by that, Arvilla," he said gravely, impressively, even warningly, "that all my life Chance has had a way of smiling on me only when the odds were badly against me. That's right where Fortune has always come in for me, and—oh, not always—no—but enough times for me to believe that— Watch out, now—for the curious pattern of *my* life. Here goes!"

Half rising out of his chair, he reached forward and cut the remaining half-deck she had left. Raised his cut section part-way up, but with the bottom-most card-face down as yet—held the section thus, a man seemingly lost in the possibilities that were inherent in this situation.

And apparently pending saying something anent it—and she was to learn almost immediately his amazing proposition, involving their both never even examining that cut deck for its bottom card!—he reached forward with his other hand, with its so-sunbrowned back, and with one simple motion of both lay the cut section momentarily in its palm, palm uppermost, yes, but the section still unexamined or unexaminable so far as bottom-most card went.

"Arvilla," he begged, letting the arm whose hand held the cut section lie on the table, seemingly as graphic emphasis for his proposition, "let's hold my cut here in *status as-is-us*—yes!—and see whether—Arvilla, can't we—right at this point—where the odds are ag'in me bad—can't we make a bargain? A bargain toward changing the terms of our wager? Deal? Bet? Or what you call it?"

"No!" she cried. "No! You're—you're not fair, Bill. I played evensteven— fair and square—made no objections to the—the weapons of our deal—yes, the weapons—cards!—and cutting same—and I got me the near-highest card of them all. And then you—you want to crawfish. I wouldn't have crawfished with you, Bill. I am Engl—that is, I am German, and would have shown the *Englisch*—that is, I would have played unqualifiedly fair and square. No bargains—had I cut, say, a deuce off-hand. Much less lost. I'd—I'd have paid—without question or cavil. I'd have—but if I won, you were to—to many me first. And—and forget this other girl. And—"

"You're making it tough," he said helplessly. "By cutting a king—and in diamonds to boot—first thing of all. You—oh, well." He shook his head. "I suppose I've caught a trey or a four-spot, or a Don't tell me—that's all."

He lifted the cut deck from the palm where it had lain during the entire discussion—held it up, bottommost card exposed to her only.

"Oh!" she cried. "Oh!" And again, "Oh!"

For the "pattern of his life" had spoken!

He had it.

The Ace of Diamonds.

He'd—he'd topped her.

She could have cried. Instead she said, "Damn! Oh, damn. Oh—"

Unbelievingly, he turned the cut deck about enough to look at it himself. Even shook his head, a man plainly stunned.

"I'm sorry, Arvilla," he said. "It's—it's the fortunes of war."

"Yes," she sighed. "It's even Dame Good-Fortune speaking to *me*—I guess. For if you had to cut cards to get out of marrying me, you—you sure didn't love me. No! Weren't within a mile of it, And if you didn't love me—what good could have come from it all? Well, I said I would play fair and square and honestly and aboveboard on this thing. Well, the name of the American woman is Mrs. Sarah Leatherberry, and she lives in the town of Middletown, Michigan."

"Middletown—Michigan?" he repeated. "Leatherberry? Mrs. Sarah Leather—you're not—"

"Call her up from here by trans-Atlantic phone," she said proudly. "And confirm it. It's all on the house!"

"No." He shook his head. "I wouldn't insult you by doing anything like that. Thank you, Arvilla—for being a real sport. And over in America that would mean—sportsman. Yes. You're a lady and a sportsman both, Arvilla. You're—I'll never forget—may I go now?"

She nodded sadly.

And relinquishing the quarter-deck which he had been holding, face uppermost, all the time, he reached down to the floor for his hat, then arose. Stood a second undecidedly. Rounded the table to where she too had arisen, and stood by her chair. He paused a moment. Then, putting his hat the only place where his hands could be free—atop his head, but tilted grotesquely to one side!—he drew her taffy-thatched head over to him. And as she closed her eyes, she felt his kiss full and warm and long on her forehead. A second later, released, and the sound of the room door gently closing in her ears, her eyes opened again, she was alone. Quite alone!

"Damn!" she said now. "But I was certain I had him. With that King of Diamonds I took off the bottom while he was all mired up checking Papa's features with respect to mine—and lay inside the deck with a hair of an edge sticking out! Why, I—I was as good as a declared winner on that. I—damn! That 'pattern of his life' sure is a pattern—and I don't mean maybe!"

But Arvilla would have been surprised indeed, had she, at this instant, heard the mental ruminations of Mr. William T. Chattock as he stepped forth from the entrance of No. 17 Furness Street, Liverpool, and closed the street door gently behind him. And which ran:

"What a little slicker she was!" he was saying to himself, though not unadmiringly by any means. "To have put that King of Diamonds, that I kept ever on the underside when I riffled those pasteboards squarely at her—inside that waiting deck. Where she could find it with her li'l finger-tippies! Boy, oh, boy—I didn't think it of her!"

And right there Mr. Chattock, turning eastward on the flagstone pavement to get to Waltham Road and the bus back to the city, was grimacing.

"But what a skunk *I* was," he was now saying ruefully, "to get the Ace of Diamonds out of that deck while she was out getting that brandy, and to palm it in my left hand, face down. And then to later slap that cut section of mine atop it—while I jockeyed with her for a better bargain. And to finally produce the whole—Acey-Facey up! I—" He shook his head contritely. "Well, that's what comes when one associates with Jules DiValo, sleight-of-hander and master of illusions. Jules DiValo who—Jules!—oh Lord, I've got to work fast. For he's—he's taking my gal. My gal! Faster, Brother Chattock, faster!"

CHAPTER VII

THE 6 YELLOW SHEETS

Pardoll Leatherberry, in his woven willow wheelchair at the end of the big capacious screened-in front porch, and smoking his huge calabash pipe, watched curiously the man in the purple corduroy trousers and belted-in blue shirt who worked away at the long unpainted, unfinished porch table at the further end. A daily leaf-calendar facing Pardoll from that end of the porch gave forth the date of June the 11th, and the generous fringe of cool shade lying out from the porch on the sunbaked grass outside showed the hour to be well past mid-afternoon. Leatherberry himself was in his grey-corded faded blue bathrobe, extra long so as to shield his lower legs, withered from early infantile paralysis; he was cleanly shaven, and his greyed hair was brushed back from his brows. The visitor worked with sheets of yellow paper laid out in a horizontal row—one Beowulf—and one atlas!

Outside the screened-in porch flowed the life of a small town. For the street outside was but of dirt, and the sidewalks of neat wooden planks. Across the way were wooden houses painted a brilliantly clean white, all of them, that one colour which can persist only in a small town.

As the young man working at the table suddenly blew out his breath in irritation as some clue apparently evaporated, Pardoll ventured to make an amused comment.

"No results yet, eh, Mr. Chattock?"

"Not yet," said the other, gazing along the line of 16 yellow sheets laid out in front of him. Pardoll took a puff on his calabash pipe. "Those six sheets hold, I take it, the six lines *you're* confident must contain the coded state and town? Now mind you," he added quickly, "I'm asking no questions. All you've told me is that an actor once spied in one of the lines of that book—a line such as *he* would have liked to have uttered on the stage!—the letters in sequence comprising the city and state which held—alas, you've told me no more, but my guess is that he had a safety-box somewhere in that city, and that today his wife—perhaps your sister?—wants to locate his private papers?"

"Not a half bad guess, Mr. Leatherberry," said Chattock, facing about. "I suppose, you being so kind, whilst your mother is visiting in the next state, I should have given you *all* the details, and—"

"Nonsense," said Leatherberry. "A man who went clear to Liverpool only to have to come back clear to Middletown, would—man, what a hop!—no wonder you pounded your ear so religiously from 11 P.M. last night, when you got off that Clipper at Chicago, that you nearly missed the 8 A.M. train out this morning for Middletown here. Now those six sheets— rather, as I chanced to see, those vertical lines cutting down through the very middle of the single line lying on each—do you mind—"

"Not at all. The way I look at it, Mr. Leatherberry, it's almost a mathematical certainty that since letters comprising the city and state lie in the line in order—in whatever line they lie in, that is—then the last two letters of the state must certainly at least fall in the last half of the line—or does that sound fallacious?"

"Heavens, no! I'd say that it was mathematical certainty. Then you're trying out the last two letters of all the states—in the last half of each line? And—"

"—and eliminating states, and in some cases—though but tentatively— lines themselves," said the young man. With a fleeting tableward glance to see what he was doing, he tapped three yellow sheets which lay to the left of his line of six. "If my hypothesis is right," he went on, "those three lines are out. For their latter halves—yes, the latter halves of all—do *not* include the last *2* letters of *any* state. Though of course I'm not discarding them. For city and state both could still be in the first half of any line. I will later probably detach the last quarter of the first half of each line, and with those six segments only, go all through my trial-and-error process again. And—all clear?"

"All clear," laughed Pardoll, blowing out a couple of whiffs of smoke, "except how do you know you're not on a false chase as to lines themselves? There are a good many lines in that work! And you have there—six. And—" He stopped.

"Oh," laughed the newcomer, "I think there's no doubt I've got *the* six lines! You see, an actor likes to see himself orating not only in front of an audience but in front of a big stage assembly. And the line he'd most read, and roll over his lips, and re-read, in his first reading of Beowulf would be the opening line of a speech, held as I've described. Yes, I simply combed out the situations wherein a male speaker orated in front of a whole stageful of characters—and took the first opening line of each!—and—well, one such situation, inaugurated in this particular work with the word 'then,' was—"

He reached slowly back of himself to the Beowulf lying open on the rear part of the table, and now, revolving completely half way round in his chair to face Pardoll Leatherberry, read aloud:

> *"Then entered therein the chief of the thanes*
> *the man brave in deeds, and honoured by fame,*
> *the stout man of war, and greeted Hrothgar.*
> *And then was brought in to the floor of the hall,*
> *where men used to drink, Grendel's head by the hair,*
> *a dread thing to view for the earls and the queen.*
> *This strange gruesome sight the men gazed upon there."*

The renderer looked up inquiringly.

"Yea!" said Pardoll. "I get it. The whole court assembled there. Stagey, *that* scene, as all get-out."

"So think I," was all the visitor would reply, and dryly. "Well, the sound-track on said scene is preceded by the words:

> *"Then speak Beowulf, son of Ecgtheow."*

He looked up.

"Yes," nodded Pardoll, "this is where the actor would commence to see himself,"

"And then," went on the man with the Beowulf, "the lines:

> *"We have brought thee with joy, o son of Healfdene*
> *and lord of the Scyldings, this spoil from the water*
> *which here thou dost look on, in token of tri—"*

The wearer of the purple corduroy trousers looked up. "That," he finished, "is how I selected my six lines." He reached back of himself and set the book over on the rear part of the table again. "It was like the half-wit who found the lost horse when everybody else had failed. By simply figuring where he would have gone had he been a horse! I just figured what line *I'd* have rolled over my thespian lips—had *I* been an actor. But—back to work!"

He revolved half about to the table again. And proceeded for some time with his now partly intelligible operations. At least he went steadily from line to atlas, atlas to line. And then—"

"Whoops!" he said. "Two click. Hold ever'thing!" And then—

"All four in it! It *must* be it. It—"

He drew forth a single yellow sheet, and took, as Pardoll could see by his very emphatic ticking-off of the endmost letter in its line lying nearest to Pardoll, its first letter for some kind of checking. Ran through the atlas. Shook his head. "No dice!"

But apparently not daunted, the man at the table, ticking off another letter right alongside the one he'd already ticked off, took the second letter of the line for checking. And repeated his search in the atlas.

Now he had his finger on the atlas column, and fixed his eyes on the line. Then eyes to column—eyes to line. And then he audibly gasped.

"Got it!" he said. "Got it! The line that contains town and state both! And what a town. No bigger than a mosquito's eye. It's it. Man, oh man—but I made it. Made it—in 2—no, about 3 hours flat!"

He closed the atlas with a resounding clap, and then in turn the small Beowulf, and lay the latter reverently atop the bigger book. He put the yellow sheets together in a heap, and came over to where Pardoll sat.

"Thank you a million, Mr. Leatherberry. I hate to run off like this, but I'm terribly behind, for this is the 11th of June, and on the 13th a certain—Mr. Leatherberry, it wasn't a safety-box I was after. I was after—believe it or not—the location of a church where a man married a girl—a girl named Mary Smith. And now—now I'm going. So I can vamoose out of here eastward—by that one late afternoon train, For I've got territory to cover! If—thank you a million."

Pardoll looked up at the other. "Well," was all he could say, "I *am* surprised. Though I don't know exactly what at. Merely, I guess, that mother's acquisition of that erratic little book in Liverpool should turn out to be a help to a—but from what line—did you get what you sought for?"

"Oh, the line? Well, since all Beowulfs are the same so far as the story and situations go, it's the first line of the situation where all the king's horses, and all the king's men—Tom, Dick, and Harry and all their brothers!—and the Scylding queen included!—are assembled in the hall of—it's right at one of those various places where the erratic translator went over to wide-measure for no discernible reason at all—it commences—"

And he repeated the simple line, though haltingly, as though not fully certain he was correct as to all the words:

> *"Then the hall was filled full of the clamour of menand*
> *Wealtheow spake—said before the whole band—"*

"I remember that scene well," nodded Pardoll. "It—and what comes next? It—it starts out, of course, 'O Beowulf,' but just what—"

The visitor made a facetious little gesture with his finger that said, "Hold ever'thing." Went back to the table he had deserted. Extracted the secondmost sheet of yellow paper. Came back with it. And handed it to Pardoll. Who examined it with interest. It read:

O Beowulf, loved youth, derive joy from this ring and with it
good luck.

"And the American town and state whose letters, are right there, in sequence, in that line are—"

"Hold everything," said Leatherberry. "I'm a lonely man. With not much to entertain myself. I'll work it out myself. After you're gone!"

CHAPTER VIII

MYSTIFIED, ONE CLERGYMAN

Floyd, Ohio!

That was the name, in faded gold-leaf letters on a black-painted background, on the sign lying over the small red-painted depot, which, at this moment—but greatly reduced in size—was all of Floyd, Ohio, that could be seen by the Reverend Jonathan Whitsitt of the Church of Our Lord, some distance off the edge of that town. For the simple reason that the young clergyman in his black robes was, at this second, peering through a tiny chink in one of the stained-glass windows of the church, where a piece of the coloured glass had fallen out.

Now, turning inward toward the little church behind him, with its heavy curved wooden beams overhead, its rows of shiny darkwood pews and its episcopalian-like altar up front over which the young blond clergyman presided on Sundays, he turned off the lights and, moving off from the window by half a dozen feet, went through a small, pulpit-like, narrow, arched wooden door, which put him in a small, cork-paved, corridor-like enclosed passage, with panes of thick, barely translucent glass built at various points along its ceiling for light, and which would carry him to his own quarters in the rectory building, off from the church.

But he did not traverse the whole 15 feet or so of the closed and eerily-lighted passage, but stopped midway, and opened another little door exactly like the one he'd just come through, which revealed a small square room, also carpeted in cork, with a single generous skylight in its ceiling, made of highly translucent stained-glass squares, which threw the early afternoon sunlight upon the interior of the room in the form of warm parallelograms of yellow, orange, lavender.

In the room were but few pieces of furniture. A light movable Bible-stand in one corner, on rollers, and bearing a huge brass-bound Bible on its wooden flanges. Two leather-seated chairs, all in all, of the most ancient vintage. A small carved table of dark wood, also on rollers, and carrying a huge leather-bound book. And on the wall across from the door a row of books, identically bound.

A man sat at the rolling table, perched forward upon one of the ancient and leather-seated chairs. Upon him, and the book before him, poured a particular warm area of yellow light. The man wore purple corduroy pants that showed black areas where certain coloured lights impinged weirdly on them, and a soft blue shirt and knitted grey tie partly encased in a considerably wrinkled blue serge coat. The Reverend Whitsitt noted, too, as he quietly closed the little door behind him, that the man had turned the single large page which the Reverend had, a little while before, found for him—a page carrying at the bottom of its scroll-adorned and curlicue-ornamented combined prayer and announcement, the names of one, Paul G. Ashbrooke, and one, Mary Smith, in their own handwritings—had turned the page and was studying some writing, or inscription, on the other side. Had, in fact, in his hands, a little device of cardboard wheels or discs.

"The inscription on the back intrigues you, I see," ventured the Reverend Whitsitt. The man looked up. "We-ell, not particularly, no. Outside of the mere fact that this girl who is so anxious to get record of her parents' marriage—that her own father has made it."

The Reverend nodded.

"It was a quaint procedure invented," he said, "by the pastor several behind me. Old Reverend Fothergill. At least, so the facts were recounted to me by the pastor from whom I took over here. Fothergill deemed that *the* place to set down family records was on the backs of these pages. Since each page, carrying but two names, sort of—of starts a new family, as it were! Yes, he deemed that to be quite an idea, since the church and rectory, being of stone, were virtually fireproof. Now and then during the years, as you may have noted, people *have* taken advantage of it. Often in code, as you'll also note."

"Which," commented the young man in front of the book, "I'll wager most of them have forgotten?"

"I doubt it not," said the Reverend. "Even if what was set down was of much interest later, in the light of babies and what-not."

He stood, hesitatingly.

"By the way, sir, I did not get time to tell you—but did you know you can get a photostat of this page for the young lady?"

"Why, no?" said the purple-corduroyed examiner of the book, surprised. "In a town so—why, when I saw this town, with fields coming right up all about it—and that single, lonely line of store-fronts—I didn't even believe what I'd learned at the post office at Detroit last evening—namely, that the town has direct airmail service 6 times a day from the south and southwest by way of Cincinnati—and 6 times a day from the east by way of Pittsburgh."

"You mean," said the clergyman, "airmail drop—*if* and *when* there ever is anything to drop!—from the busy Southern-Eastern Air Service. Well that, my friend, is something that arises out of the history of airmail in the United States. It's a—a sort of a gesture, commemorating the fact that 'way back, almost in the days of the Wright Brothers—but I won't try to outline it."

"Well, drop or not," said the stranger, "and commemorative or not—it's airmail service—to *me!* For—but now about that photostating? Do you really mean to say that in such a small town as this I can—"

He had stopped, still plainly incredulous.

And the Reverend Whitsitt, who had not always himself been of Floyd, Ohio, took up valiantly in his defence of this town of which he was now a more or less permanent fixture.

"Yes, I do. And I should have told you that when I left you here, after getting down what appeared to be the proper volume of those marriage-register books, and finding for you what appeared to be the proper page. Yes, you can have a photostat of either or both sides of that page made. There is a young chap uptown who has a portable photostating machine, and does many documents for the county. It will be no more than a dollar and a half each side. And you could have them in an hour."

"That's—that's scrumptious. Thanks a lot. And I'll be tickled stiff if you'll phone for him. Meanwhile, till he comes, I'll just play along with this stuff on the back and this little set of wheels—if you don't mind? I may as well fetch the young lady anything her father wrote—in his own phraseology."

"Of course. Of course. Well, while I phone over to Charlie Satterlee, can I do anything else for you? Like—well, phoning some telegram or something that you'd like to have in transit while you do the other things?"

"We-ell," was the stranger's puzzled reply, "I hardly know what to say. I'm expecting an airmail letter before I leave here. Thanks to the fact that there appears to be lively air-service between a certain airfield where a letter of mine, written at Detroit, went, and from which reply will come. It—well about all I could logically wire now, I guess, would be the old cliché 'disregard letter—data set forth in it was all wrong.' In short, I wonder if I could perhaps have been—ah—haywire, on certain air routes out of Columbus and Cincinnati in this state?"

"Columbus? And Cincinnati?" The Reverend smiled reassuringly. "Well I was secretary to the Bishop in a large church in each of those cities before I was assigned here. Handling, in each case, all sorts of important church mail, and routing out officials of the church who had to pass through to—now if it comes to routes out of either city to *anywhere,* I think I am pretty well informed."

"Reverend, you're the answer today to everything in a man's life! For—well, would you mind reading the carbon copy of a letter I hammered out in a Detroit hotel room last night and check me if anything in it seems ridiculous? I mean—as to the connections described in it, and even as to whether the recipient could reach me back here today with an airmail reply?"

"Gladly," said the clergyman. "So long as there's nothing in your letter that's private. Since I will have to take the non-time-table stuff with the timetable stuff, not so? Gladly."

The stranger was already withdrawing from his breast pocket some papers of various sorts, including, as the clergyman saw, a small, narrow, green, cloth-bound book which he was shortly to learn, from the letter itself, was a route-book, showing the daily changing location of a travelling show, as well as even the hours of departure and arrival. From the papers, the stranger extracted a tri-folded one which evidently constituted the carbon of his discussed letter. Shoving everything else back, including the green book, he rose and came over to the Reverend Whitsitt with the paper.

The clergyman took it, and the stranger, evidently not wishing to stand over him like an avenging angel compelling speed, dropped back in his chair again.

The letter, Whitsitt saw, as he first examined carefully its address and addressee in order to better pass verdict on its deliverability and answerability, if not what travel connections might be mentioned in it, comprising several sheets rather than one, had been sent to one Angus MacWhorter, of "The MacWhorter Mammoth Motorized Shows." To and at a town in a far-distant southwest state called just Pricetown. The letter ran:

Dear Mr. MacWhorter,

This highly optimistic bit of letter-writing is postulated on the glowing, roseate theory that you will receive it tomorrow morning at Pricetown, at or near the moment you yourself are pulling in there. Assuming that it actually does reach you, I shall be out of Detroit where I am at the moment, and working on toward a town in Ohio called Floyd. Where I definitely can get an airmail reply from you containing any instructions you may have in line *with,* or counter *to,* my plans once I leave there. I can get your airmail reply to this letter if sent by you immediately, routed via Cincinnati—remember *that: Cincinnati*—addressed me "care The Mansion House" at Floyd, and made, of course, special-delivery.

Now my plans will then and thereupon involve exclusively the matter of my delivery of some rare bacon in person. The point is that since I shall then be in Ohio, considered to be the crossroads for certain airlines heading southwestward in various directions, I am in a most fortuitous position for quickly rejoining you at any part of the territory, airportless though that territory is for the most part—and airserviceless practically completely as well. Not only that, but I shall be in perfect position for seeing Krantz

Altergott, your circus wagon maker in Columbus, Ohio, about that special trailer you've had in mind—"

Here a humble tap on the door back of the Reverend Whitsitt arrested his reading of the letter. Letter in hand, he turned and went over to the door and opened it.

It was Cubie—the middle-aged Negro who did the porter work about the rectory and the church.

"Rev'n Whitsitt," he said, "dey is two aihmails done des come fo' you—one f'm Chy-cago—by way ob Toledo—and one f'm No'fo'hk, 'Ginia—by way ob Cinci."

"Thank you, Cubie."

Cubie, passing a black hand over his ebony-black forehead, withdrew. The Reverend Whitsitt bent his attention to the letter again, which resumed:

> For my plans, Mr. MacWhorter, after finishing what I propose to do in Floyd, Ohio, are as follows: I shall leave from Floyd by Yankee Bus Lines bus in early evening for Columbus, Ohio, from where I can fly at midnight on a freight-plane of the Western Freight Transport Lines, and from which I can get myself set down on a certain lonely airfield in Kansas, called Tall Grass Airfield. I can then go by a train of the Kansas and Northeastern Oklahoma Railroad to a point 6 miles west of Foleysburg, the day-after-tomorrow's show-point, and walk in the 6 miles or so via shanks' mare to the show, some couple of hours ahead of show-close. If, however, Mr. MacWhorter, you want that Siamese-twin mummy checked up on, and negotiated for, in Cinci, I can easily equally well reach Cincinnati from here by fast train, have a couple of hours there, and go out by a most scrumptious sleeper-plane of the Cincinnati-El Paso Lines which can get me to Pricetown. A fact. Absolutely a fact, Mr. MacWhorter, unbelievable as it sounds to you. I can get to Pricetown by a Southern Trailways Bus by 8 A.M. which, according to the route-book, will be precisely 5 hours after the show itself has departed. In which case, therefore, you will of course have to arrange to leave one "wagon" behind, so that I may be thus myself transported show-ward and land at Foleysburg myself about 5 hours after you do, which should be 5 P.M. But again—in perfect time for my up-and-at-'em-boys-and-over-the-wall act.
>
> The only point at issue, Mr. MacWhorter, is that I want to do my "marines act" in person—not by crosscountry telephoning to the show, see?—yes, that rare bacon delivery—which means I *must* hook on to the route at or ahead of Foleysburg—ahead of show-close there—but in no event beyond. No not beyond! So airmail me immediately your prefer-ence—*if* any!— instructions likewise—*if* any!—and if same are received any time up to my pulling out from Floyd, I'll do all I can to make my plans fit yours. Thanks a million.
>
> Bill Chattock.

The clergyman looked up from the long letter with a smile.

"You are correct entirely on all these air-routes out from both Columbus and Cincinnati," the Reverend now said. 'Though as to whether your letter, sent from Detroit, ever reaches your circus-proprietor employer, I couldn't in slightest degree venture. Well, for your nerves' and bones' sake, I hope your employer wants the mummy found, instead of the wagon-maker talked to!" He smiled again. "Well, I'll get hold of Charlie Satterlee at once."

And saluting jovially with his two fingers, the Reverend turned, opened the pulpit-topped door at his side, and went out, closing the little door gently behind him. Though outside in the eerily-lighted passageway that would now take him to his own quarters, and to the telephone, he shook his head helplessly.

"Odd," he ruminated. "That Foleysburg business! What on earth, I wonder, can happen at the close of show in that little town which is so—so supremely important in his life? I wonder? What—oh, well!"

CHAPTER IX

THE MAN WITH THE RED NOSE

"Spearfish" Meldrum, tramp telegraph operator in the town of Price-town, sourly regarded the long folded oblong of flimsy paper that had been accidentally dropped to the floor by the tall, kindly-looking circus-proprietor with the swallowtail coat and the silk hat, who had just filed a wire and departed.

Spearfish's sour demeanour in the direction of the long folded paper he'd picked up was because the tall, kindly, silk-hatted man who had inadvertently lost it represented Capital, which Spearfish—representing "Labour," according to his own views!—devoutly hated. The filed wire itself gave but little clue to the very interesting—most interesting, indeed!—facts that Spearfish was shortly to find in and on the folded oblong. For, addressed to a man named Chattock in a spit of a town called Floyd, Ohio, it had but said:

> In case my airmail sent early today does not reach you, come via Cincinnati-Pricetown route exactly as you outlined. See Banker Hickory Noon who, on identification of yourself by Karl the Klown, who will be there, will explain a certain set-up. If letter is received okay, and all is in order, wire me single word "Confirmed."
>
> MacWhorter.

If Spearfish had been but helping out here for a few hours today, instead of covering the office all by himself, he would have asked for time off, clapped on his hat hurriedly, and gone down to the lot where the circus was, returned the doubtlessly worthless bit of flimsy paper to the proprietor with much flourish and eloquence, and made the—the son-of-a-capitalistic bitch kick in with a couple of pasteboards for the evening performance. And—but Spearfish could not leave his job. He was "main squeeze" here today. In place of Clint Harkley, the regular operator. For Spearfish, having knocked at the rear window this morning for a job while *en route* from Bubbling Springs City, to the east of Pricetown, to California-or-bust, had been given a 24-hour stretch, at 36 hours' pay, since much wiring would be done tonight, with the town full of visitors. But because the paper in his hand belonged to Capital—might even contain some state secret because of which Capital would be glad to pay $5 to Labour to get it back!—Spearfish unfolded it, and proceeded to see what it might possibly hold within itself.

It comprised, he saw as he unfolded it, two sheets of paper and not one, so flimsy was the material in each. They were, as he also saw immediately, the carbon copy of a typewritten letter. The same airmail letter, plainly, mentioned in the wire just filed directed to the man Chattock. And Spearfish read with widening eyes, as he began to see that he, Spearfish Meldrum, was becoming possessed of a secret that few persons in the Universe right now had! The letter started out simply enough. With no out-and-out mention of the secret it contained. Its recipient was evidently much loved by its sender. The letter ran:

William T. Chattock,
Mansion House,
Floyd, Ohio.

Manna from heaven, boy, your airmail letter from Detroit! At this juncture of my affairs, anyway! So much so that I shall slap this reply back on the airways for Floyd, Ohio. Where I do hope I can catch you.

Well, Bill, since you are in Ohio—and *can* reach Cincinnati by fast train, and *can* go out of there tonight by sleeper plane, and, thanks to a lonely refuelling "must" field, can have yourself set down south of Pricetown, I want you to forego entirely this dubious combination of hops you propose to make via that Kansas route, plus jerkwater train to west of Foleysburg. So, Bill, take that Cinci route—yes—and put yourself into Pricetown tomorrow morning via Nosebag Field exactly as you've outlined, and all of which *is* in the bag for you—for 8 A.M.

Now there will not be a held-back vehicle and driver waiting for you, for the sad and simple reason that I'm hopelessly up against it for drivers. No, what I want you to do is to pick up a certain truck that will be waiting here for you. And which you will find, under guard, at—listen, Bill, when you've perused this letter, destroy it immediately and completely, even 'way up there in Ohio. Burn it up right away, yes.

Now the truck I want you to pick up is right now locked in the garage of Pricetown's bank president Hickory Noon, under surveillance of Karl the Klown, who will sleep in there tonight with it, for general safety's sake. Its left rear wheel is badly smashed from a collision with a tractor, coming into Pricetown. It had to be dragged in the rest of the way, on skids. Yes, it's the big white office truck, Bill, minus the usual pictorial emblems and carrying only the name of the shows, and containing our National Money Transportation Company's funds-deposit-safe concealed in its rear end. And which is now waiting a new wheel, of its confounded outsize type, due down tomorrow on the 11 A.M. train from Wheel City, south of here. Karl, after putting on the wheel, and in turn identifying you to Banker

Noon, will turn the truck over to you, and will go into the local hospital here for an operation that positively can't wait.

Now you proceed immediately to follow us over the route. You will be running no more than 9 hours or so behind us, since pull-out from Pricetown is always at 3 A.M. The covering of the route, the greater part of which lies through so-called Idiot's Valley—a tortuous drive, yes, but with no errors possible due to its having only the one road, Old Twistibus—shouldn't take you a bit more than the 9 hours or so it will take us. If as much, since you'll be travelling out-of-train. Indeed you'll be heading into Idiot's Valley about the very time we are commencing to unload at Foleysburg. And so you should be in Foleysburg before dark, at very latest. Long before, you see, show even technically opens, let alone closes. Which appears to be what you want, for reasons I can't fathom.

Now, Bill, keep your eye on the ball! Because the bank president back in Emory City, who was agent for the system protecting our safe, had lost his code-book the night before in a fire—and couldn't open the combination, varying by clockwork with the date, with only his key; while this Pricetown banker, Hickory Noon, has a defective key—and *it* won't open up the safe, even though the combination appears right for this particular date. Hence, there is nearly three thousand dollars cash money accumulated in that safe, which will not be openable, and its contents depositable, before you bring it into Foleysburg, where the bank has a code-book, and of course will have a perfect key! Just tell anyone from whom you have to make any inquiries about the road ahead of you that you are a straggler car, catching up with the outfit, and if they inquire specifically—as they usually do—as to what is in the truck, just say it contains costumes needed for the grand ensemble. Or rigging for a high-wire act. Or both! The secret of its contents—for Karl believes there to be only five or six hundred dollars running funds in the safe—are exclusively in the possession of myself, Banker Noon, and now—*you.* Now about Melody, I can tell you little. She's not even in yet, for the most of the show is rolling along an hour behind the first few cars in one of which I am. All I can tell you is that she has been somewhat sad up to some days ago, but about then seemed to have come to a sudden firm decision about something. What it is, I cannot say. But since she's promised to stay with me till she's 21, and that's not till close-of-show tomorrow Friday the 13th, and you'll be here long, long before, you can ask her yourself. Confirm all this, please, and your acceptance in full of the instructions, by the single wired word "Confirmed."

MacWhorter.

PS. Of course, Bill, should you suffer any unforeseen delays along your trek—a thing that *can* happen!—delays from double tyre blow-ups—piston-ring or spark-plug breakdowns or what, I expect you to forego your less important matter of rejoining ahead of Foleysburg show-close, and to just keep trailing along on to Spottsville. Just stay with the truck always, in person, that's all. But I'm sure you'll rumble in at Foleysburg okay.

A. MacW.

Spearfish, coming to the end of the long letter, had but one dazed comment to make.

"Oh, boy!" he ejaculated. "Has—has this baby got a state's secret! Three grand laying in a little old truck from which it can't be extracted—oh boy!—This in response to a new thought. "When that Scotch son-of-a-bitch finds this is gone, he'll be back like the north wind, and then—"

And here it was that Spearfish, even not yet ticking on all fours, had a sudden hunch. To do something, the reason for which was not altogether clear to him. For, folding the pair of carbon-imprinted sheets up, page 1 back on top, he rounded the counter through the small swinging gate, lay the oblong on the floor in front of the counter exactly where the tall silk-hatted customer had stood, and over it draped carelessly a copy of the today's *Bi-weekly Peckham County Argus.* It was a copy he had earlier placed on the counter, after the departure of the circus-proprietor, for any belated non-paper-buyer to take. And back he went quickly to his sending table, just in time to see what he'd anticipated materialize! For the street door was darkened by the same tall, silk-hatted man in the frocktail coat, coming in.

"I beg pardon, young man," he boomed, "but did you find anything on the floor in there?"

Spearfish cast a glance toward and along the inner face of the counter rail. "Nothing in here, sir. And if it's not out there, then—"

"There's only a copy of a newspaper there," said the circus-proprietor disgruntledly.

"Oh, paper? Well, that was fetched in right after you left, and slid off as the man who filed it left here. Do you mind handing it to me?"

"Not at all," came the response of the Scotchman, Came forward, raised up the paper, and—

"Why, here it is!" he cried. "My letter."

"Well," said Spearfish dryly, but without coming forward, like a busy, busy man, "now you know how it is! You do a good deed—and you get rewarded. Glad you got it back, sir. Just leave it there on the counter if you will. Thanks."

"And you come to see the show this evening," said the circus-proprietor. "I'll be taking the tickets myself tonight. I'll pass you, and any lady you bring."

"Thanks, mister, but I'm on this job for 24 hours."

The big Scotchman, nodding, ambled away, restoring his oblong of paper to his breast pocket. Now Spearfish, entirely alone, sat in a daze, his brain a chaos of conflicting thoughts.

"It's—it's too perfect," he said. "It's too perfect. First time in my life I ever hooked on to a piece o' inside info like that—even handling countless thousands of wires."

And shaking his head because of the sheer impossibility of a man doing other than what he was about to do, he drew over a sheet of yellow manilla paper, and proceeded, with his soft pencil, to write out upon it a telegram. When he finished his wire, he took from his hip pocket a small, red-cloth-bound pocket dictionary of a kind to be found all over the U.S.A., thanks to the fact that it was handled by the 5- and 10-cent stores of all chains. Looking up in it a certain word, he glanced at the wall to make sure it *was* the 12th of the month—then counted 12 words ahead. With which he wrote the code word "Slip"—but preceded by the hyphenated prefix "co" to show it really was code—above the uncoded word "Sheer." Swiftly he went through the message, leaving all harmless words uncoded, but coding all meaningful ones.

Now he counted off his message as a day-letter, then counted his coded words, at 2 cents each, and without consulting rate-book or what, figured mentally—then rose from his chair and went to the counter, where he placed in the till—but not without a pained scowl—the sum of $1.75. Now he carefully read his wire. Not as coded, no—but as originally written. It ran:

Day-letter, coded words extra,

Studd Bowersix,
Hogan's Railroad Hotel,
Bubbling Springs City.

Slicer, a white circus truck carrying a standard funds-deposit safe, cleverly concealed somewhere in its rear end, but with three grand cash in it, leaves Pricetown tomorrow morning at 11 P.M. Truck is bound Foleysburg via Idiot's Valley, one driver—no guards. You and any two hard guys you can raise there in B.S.C. will have plenty of time to barge in to the Valley tonight, well ahead of it, and to lay for it in that godforsaken stretch, at the further end, ahead of the Poison Swamp. I want only my 10 per cent of the take and am passing this tip-off to you because you are 24-k and okay on that. Contact me for the wire pay-off at Kitterling's Flop, Tulsa, Oklahoma, for I am bound for California, and will be gone from here after about 2 A.M. tomorrow.

Spear.

"Oke," he said, satisfied.

And, laying the wire in front of him, he drew over, on its oiled rollers, the Hi-Speed Tape-Preparing machine. And commenced preparing the sending tape.

CHAPTER X

ONE SIDE OF NOWHERE!

Bill Chattock brought to a grinding stop the white circus truck he was driving. Ahead of him stretched the dreary, sunbaked dirt road, minus habitations, minus even fences, cooking in the vertical rays of the noonday sun. Behind him—rather, behind the gleamingly white boxlike structure on which was painted only, in flaming red letters, "MacWhorter's Mammoth Motorized Shows," lay the same dreary road, likewise minus habitations. True, there *was* one sign of life—it was the reason Bill Chattock had drawn to a stop—and that was the lone dilapidated store by the roadside, just to the right of where Bill's truck now stood.

Turning on his serge-coat-upholstered seat, he surveyed the store for signs of life. Over the narrow doorway was a roughly white-painted plank, with crude green letters that spelled ELUM'S STORE.

Now a woman appeared in the doorway of the store, gazing out curiously. She was thin, bony, high-cheeked, and clad in a drab calico dress, with her grey-black hair done up in a tight topknot on her head. Malarial yellow in colour, she was chewing a twig of sweetwood, which she had to take from her mouth to talk.

"What's a matter of ye, mister?" she said in a high cackling voice. "Lose yore show?"

"No," he said, looking down at her, almost just below him, "I'm just trailing it. Matter of some last-minute repairs that had to be made to this truck back in Pricetown."

"Whut you totin' in it?" she asked. "A whale?"

He smiled tolerantly.

"Did have a pickled midget whale in it a while back," he lied gracefully. "But now it's got just costumes, needed for the Big Splash." He told her no more. "Madame, as I came along here I saw, trailing out from your store behind, on a line of low weather-beaten poles, one phone line going to—nowhere! Now is it possible to get a long-distance connection? Or *any* connection with anywhere that can put a long-distance connection through?"

"W'y, shore you kin git a long-distance c'nnection," she said, almost indignantly. "Right on that wire itself."

"Well, can I make a long-distance call on your phone, then? And pay you, for the tolls?"

"'Co'se you kin," she said, with the high irritability of one who lived in a region where everyone's facilities were at the disposal of everybody. "'Cep'n," she added, "you've got to pay 10 p'cent of the callin' charges as a fee fer a-usin' of the phone. We don't git much bus'ness 'round hyar—jest the tricklin's in f'm th'ee diff'ent roads."

"Gladly." He quickly cut her argument off, "And this fee'll amount to something, madame! For I've got to say more than 10 words."

He swung his head out of the cab now, and gazed at the other phone line that, crossing over his machine, was disappearing over the knolls and scrub-oak patches to the left.

"Might I ask," he put in, "what that phone line connects with?" Adding, because it *was* important to him: "Some phone system, maybe?—down in Idiot's—ah—uh—Old Twistibus Valley?"

"Hah!" she cackled. "You shore hain't driv *this* route afore. Phone system—in Idjit's Valley! Them savages? Why, none of 'em wouldn't know w'ich end of a tellyphone to talk into! Much less—'sides, they hain't 'nough of 'em in the whole valley to jest'fy no phone system. Tellyphones! Why, mister, them's the most ign'ant people what ever lived anywhar in the whole world. They're so in-bred that they air swarmin' with idjits. That's w'y the route ah'id of ye is most'y called Idjit's Valley, instead o' Old Twistibus Valley like as it should."

"But that line," he asked. "It seems to go that way. What becomes of it? I ask, because if I get locomotive trouble there in that valley, I'd like to be able to—"

"Mister," she said, "ef'n you git loc'moting trouble in thar, better git it ahead of or near 5-mile p'int! Whar that thar phone line ends. Ends at a purty little white cottage builted a year ago by a mill'onaire from New York. He hadda have a phone to th' outside to git the daily market quotationin's on! He died in thar this spring, and got burrit in back. And the place got rented immed'ate to Miss Saxone Crestfield."

"Miss Sax—Saxone?—"

"The lady nov'list," the woman said proudly. "She's writin' a book now 'bout them savages livin' beyant her. 'Cep'n they don't guess it! Reckon she writes up all her male char-act-ters out'n Willie-Willie."

"Willie-Willie?"

"Mister," she laughed scornfully, "you shore air a furr'ner. I could talk to you all day 'bout them folks in the Valley ef'n you don't keer 'bout gittin' to your show."

"And," he said firmly, "that's where this baby's got to git!" He withdrew his ignition key from the instrument board in front of him. "Well, I'll make my call."

"Now wait!" the woman cautioned him sternly. "Ef'n yo're figgahin' to call Foleysburg whar yore show is 'bout now dockin', you cain't do it nohow. For I got me a sister livin' thar, an'—"

"Well, no, I wasn't. I did hear—yes, that it was minus a phone system because of some—some weird reasons connected with—but I did wonder, while I sat here, if there wasn't some single official line running in there—or—or—er—bootleg phone line—by which—"

"Good Lawdy, no!" she cried. "Them 'ligious fanatics?—what run that town? Oh," she qualified, "they ain't so much thataway today—no—for they're the 'scendants of the real 'ligious fanatic Old Man Foley whut thunk 'lectricity was the devil, an' put his views into all his land grants fer the whole caounty. Why—ef any land-owner thar runs any wire into ours out o' his propitty—or sports a raddio *on* it—he—he loses title to his land! To his neighbours—each side. Why, mister, ef'n yore own maw was a-dyin' inside that town, right now, they wouldn't be nohow way to phone in any message to nobody 'bout her. Nor to telly graft. Not even—to send a message on the raddio."

"Worse and worse!" said Bill Chattock. "Well, that conclusively means this company of marines has got to jump over the wall in person—and not by phone. And has got to watch the old gears—to boot! Well, I'll make that call now."

And he climbed down in order to make what was—in some respects, at least—the most important phone call he had ever made.

Elum's Store inside was a barren place. The walls of the store were adorned by many and various signs advertising chewing tobacco, and, piled along the base of the store's front wall, and visible to Bill only after he got inside, were several dozen of bright red 5-gallon cans—gasolene cans, full, empty or both!—showing that this place was the only kind of gas station this primitive region could boast. On the wall alongside the heavily-screened entrance door was the phone itself; old-fashioned—a brassy transmitter arm stretching forth belligerently from it, and with, on the wooden box beneath the latter, a huge crank.

He turned to the instrument, raised its receiver, and from force of habit waited. The woman, somewhere in back of him, cackled derisively.

"What'sa matter of ye, City Man? Don't ye know how to use a kentry phone? Ye gotta churn th' crank. An'—but wait."

"Yes?" His head was turned around.

"Ef Miss Crestfield answers, jest say yo're crankin' fur Cedarville. An' she'll hang up. The phones is connected on the same sarcuit, see?"

"Thanks." He turned back, and did now revolve the handle. Miss Crestfield, lady novelist, evidently was out gathering material or something—for he got a typical small-town answer in a second, in a woman's voice. And the answerer, moreover, knew from the strength of the ring, or something, *who* was cranking!

"Yessum, Mis' Elum? What kin I do fer ye?"

"What—what central am I in connection with?"

"Oh, drummer, heh? Yo're in c'nnection 'ith Cedarville, east an' north of ye."

"I see. Well Miss—ah—Mrs. Elum has given me permission to make a long-distance call. Will you get me, then, the following party? Person to person, moreover. The party is in a city called Wine City. And his name is Monteen Kirkaldy." He spelled it out. "15 West 15th Street." And now he gave the girl the city again, but gave her the far-off state it was in as well.

The girl at the other end evidently referred to some book at her elbow. For finding the rate. "That'll be three dollars fer three minutes, mister. An' 50 cents a minute tharafter. I'll call you back."

Now the phone back of him tinkled. He turned anxiously to it.

"Hy'ars yo're party, mister. Got th'ough quick by way o' Nashville, Tenn'see—thence nawth."

He heard her talking on another circuit now.

"Hyar's the party who's-a callin' of Mist' Kirk—aldy, Wine City."

There was clicking and various noises.

And now across miles of space—uncivilized space some of it, and some of it not!—came the pleasant voice of a youngish-sounding man. A voice ever so familiar to Bill Chattock, since it was that of his today-closest friend.

"Monteen Kirkaldy—speaking?"

Bill, with eyes momentarily closed, had the eerie sense, at this moment, that the slim dark-eyed Monteen was but the other side of this very wall. And opening his eyes to dispel the illusion, he got immediately down to business.

"Here's hoping that Monteen possesses, this second, the sum of $56.50 *cash money!* This is Bill Chattock speaking!"

"Bill—Chattock?" came the astounded reply. "Bill? What—in—hell! Why, I—I just got an airmail postcard from you from Liverpool."

"It travelled to you on the same plane I did. A long story, Monte. Concerned with the use of that round-trip passage prize I won. And I'll give the story to you some time when we're not on a wire."

"Okay. Well, how are you, Bill?"

"A damned—darned sight healthier than when you saw me last. Yes, my life was just about saved by the certain Mr. MacW. Who—but say, Monte, I want you to do something for me."

"Of course, of course," the other man got in. "Name it. What is it?"

"Just this, Monte. Amongst those papers of mine you're keeping for me, is a pawn-ticket for a beautiful diamond engagement ring, worth all of $250. I pawned it, for $50, about 13 months ago, just to keep it safe in a fireproof vault. Living as I was then in a firetrap. Now I've been fatuously thinking all the time that it expired on the 12th of next month. And that fool ticket, as I now calculate, expires either the 12th or 13th of *this* month. Not next month. Now it's pawned with Sol Nudelman, on White Grape Street. And—"

"I get you, Bill. You want me to skip over and pay the interest on it? Well, 13 months at the Wine City legal rate of 1 per cent per month is—is $6.50. So consider same done, and—"

"We-ell, I—I want you to do even more. If you're not broke, that is! I want you—to redeem it. If, that is, I'm not out on a limb on the—the time-angle. For Sol is a tough one. He'd foreclose on a—however, I can hope. No, I want you to redeem it, if you can, take it up street to the express office, have it crated there before your eyes in the usual jewellery box, and ship it to me—"

"Yes? I'm taking this down."

"To—well, Hootens Falls is a good contact point, since it's well ahead of me. Ahead of the show, that is. Oh, yes, I'm back with the outfit. Hootens Falls say. In the State of—"

"Oh, I know Hootens Falls! From the time, 2 years back, when I covered Kansas, Missouri, Oklahoma and Arkansaw for Cied Brothers, Cutlery, of K.C."

"Well, I'm going to ask even more of you. And it's to call me back, right where I now am, as soon as you've loped across, and put my mind to rest about that date. Lord, I'd hate to lose that ring."

"Say no more, Bill! I'll ring you back gladly. From over at the vaults. They have triple-encased booths—fine service. Where—so you're planning to desert bachelorhood, eh?—now that you have a nut-brown skin!—and muscles of steel. Okay, okay. We all do it sooner or later. Well, on the assumption that you'll get the ring back, what are you going to lay on the lady's finger *till* then?"

"Oh," laughed Bill, "I've an engagement present for *her* that'll put a look on her face ten times more ecstatic than any fool ring. Well, what were you doing when I jarred you into ring-hunting activity?"

"Glooming."

"Glooming? About what?"

"Oh, because I'd just cooked up a nice re-hash story on a famous murder case, to sell to one of the many true-crime-story magazines. The story of my re-hash was the Case of the Ragpicker Joe Murder—"

"Ragpick—Ragpicker Joe Murder—did you say?"

"We-ell, yes. Do you know anything about it?"

"We-ell, I know the story's on the stands right now in a magazine. A re-hash, that is. A—"

"Well, that's just it," returned Kirkaldy glumly. "You see, I was lucky enough, while in Chicago some time back, to pick up an unpublished photograph of this nigger, who lived in the garbage dumps there in Chi. Twenty-five long years ago, you understand. No, it wasn't the single existing standard pic of him that appears in most re-hash stories on his murder. This one I got was taken of him by a social worker, just before his murder. Well, with that pic as a bait, I expected to get $150 for my re-hash tale of it all. But, lo—the whole tale's out on the stands as happens—and my story is blotto!"

"Well," returned Bill thoughtfully, "put your story away. You—you do have the unpublished pic, you know. So put it all away—for a year. Then come to your Uncle Bill."

"Why—have you an angle, Bill?"

"Have I—an angle? Listen, Buddy-boy, I sort of—no, I do have, see? I could give you one dazzling angle alone, here and now, that would easily give a re-run of the whole story. I could keep on giving—but the inside facts I have sort of belong, just now, to a certain girl towards whom I'm heading. So put your story away, and see me in a year. For at least one good re-hash."

"That I'll do! Well, Bill, when am I going to see you? I didn't get the source of this call. I take it you're in some big city. For I seem to hear a pile-driver or something methodically driving a pile for the foundation of some huge building."

"Yeah? Well that's a dust-cloth—slapping flies—on a counter."

"The hell you say! Why it sounds exactly like—"

"Yes, that's how radio does it, too!"

"But at that you're rather close to Wine City, aren't you? For—"

"Close? Man, you'd be surprised if you knew where I was. I'm talking from a little isolated store out in a godforsaken stretch of the earth that one man in the show calls 'Little Australia.' I'm driving a truck to catch up with the outfit. I'm just about to head into a district where the road is supposed to twist and turn and wave and loop to get through the hollows and ridges and heavy growths of timber and—"

"Bill! Bill? You're not—not, by some remote chance, are you, standing in a store called—Elum's? On a—a road called—called Carthage Road East? On the edge of going into Old Twistibus?"

"Why—ah, yes. Do you know anything of Elum's—and Old Twistibus?"

"Do *I* know—anything of 'em? Lord, when I was selling goods for that K.C. firm, I drove jauntily down into Old Twistibus one day. I was in the process of trying to get from a town called Pricetown to a town called

Spottsville by way of a town where I thought I might stop off a few hours and sell a gross of knives—a town called Foleysburg. Bill, you're in the damdest cul-de-sac—pocket—trap—whatever one should call it—in the whole U.S.A.!"

"Whaddye mean—cul-de-sac? Pocket? Trap? You—you talk as though I won't even get to Foleysburg, where I'm heading right now."

"You won't," said Kirkaldy authoritatively. "No matter what golden data you're huffing and chuffing along on right now. No, you won't get to Foleysburg. Not today, tomorrow, not the next. Nor never!"

"Whaddye mean," Bill demanded irately, "that I'll—I'll never reach Foleysburg today, tomorrow—nor ever?"

"Well, the set-up is this," Kirkaldy answered. "In the first place, didn't your mama tell you nothin', when you left Pricetown or Cedarville—whichever town you did leave from, since from either you *could* have wound up there at Elum's?"

"My mammy," snapped Bill, considerably disconcerted by the cool comments of the other, "was a very worried clown—one who was all jittered about a simple operation he had to have—who merely turned over a white truck to me, back in Pricetown, and said—oh, sure, he did give me a suspicious 'God bless you' at that. H'm? But what do you mean—I won't ever reach Foleysburg?"

"I mean this," suddenly snapped Kirkaldy; "you're facing the unskirtable but at the same time impossible Mud River—no bridges for hundreds of miles down. Even if you could reach it from where you are, which you couldn't, for the reason that there are no roads to it, and only swamps along its edge. And at right angles to you—though all of 50 miles or so ahead—beyond some dried mud flats is Smoky Mountain Range. And—but the point I'm trying to get at is that between the Mountain end—or the Mountain and Escarpment, as you wish—and the River—is your Old Twistibus Valley.

"And so," concluded Kirkaldy, "thar hain't no way around old Twistibus Valley leftwise—because of Mud River, with no road to, nor bridge across. And," went on Kirkaldy, actually singing his description now in hillbilly intonations, "ain't no way araou-ou-ound the Valley right'ard!—because of Smoky Range—with no passes through it for some hundreds of miles. And there's no way whatsoever to get further west, from where you now stand and fume, except by way of a road that is said to have evolved from an Indian trail called Crazy Snake Trail, though I personally believe it was once laid out by a drunken knitress with the soul of the Devil in her—no way, except through hillbilly-mountaineer-river-bottom people who—"

"Hillbilly?—mountaineer?—river-bottom—what do you mean, Monte? And stop your damned facetiousness. This—this is serious to me. If you know *something*—go on? What do you mean?"

"Why, I mean, you will now proceed to do what your Uncle Monte will tell you to do! In short, you will turn ri-i-ight around where you are now, see? And will go back to Pricetown. No—wait! You'll have a nice sleep there tonight. And just before dawn tomorrow, you'll bowl straight southward to Mud River. Reaching thus a place called Sunrise Sam's Ferry. Where an old galoot with a 6-foot-long beard and a flatboat operating on a cable by a hand-winch, comes over each day at sunrise from some cove on the opposite side, and takes back a few cars. Sunrise Sam is his name, as you can guess, and he was written up only last week in the *Saturday Evening Post*. You'll thus get across this barrier, see. And—no wait! And over in that yander state—on t'other side, you'll bowl merrily westward till you finally come to a highway called—'at's right—the Foleysburg-Spottsville Road! Where you could turn right and finally roll into Foleysburg. Only you'll turn left, of course, and wind up at a town called Spottsville. And thus you see," showed Mr. Kirkaldy triumphantly, "you'll never see Foleysburg tonight, tomorrow, nor never."

"My fine router of man and beast over turnpike and coachroad," chided Bill sadly, "who has consumed several dollars' time on this wire for which I shall have to pay this very estimable lady here 10 per cent commission—but far worse, have lost some of my valuable driving time across this—this Dale of the Dead—I am *not* bound for Spottsville. Through Foleysburg. I am going to Foleysburg."

"You—you don't mean," stammered Kirkaldy, "that your outfit is playing *that* town?"

"Yes. Why not?"

"Good Lord! I didn't dream—MacWhorter Micro-cosmic Shows, eh, instead of Mammoth? I didn't—still, why don't you pass it up?"

"Listen, I have to be at Foleysburg before show-close tonight. My gal is taking it on the heel-and-toe with a wax-moustached villain. Atop of which, serious business has to be transacted in Foleysburg by MacWhorter with—with some papers I'm carrying through for him, see? It can't be done elsewhere, see? It's—it's just got to be done at Foleysburg."

"You win! You win," retorted Kirkaldy. "Then there's nothing on God's green earth you can do, of course—if you have to get there—and get there tonight—but to keep right on going. Nose on the road. But fortunately for you—one road only."

"That's a-a-all I want to know," said Bill Chattock. "I'll be in Foleysburg by dusk tonight."

"You will," said Mr. Kirkaldy, radiating good cheer, "if you don't have a breakdown at—say—Middle Point. If you do, you'll be all of two full days walking out of the valley. In *any* direction at all! For from around there it's all of 30 or more miles—as a crow flies, that is—and only a guide could pilot you from road-bend to road-bend—all of 30 miles in all directions to anywhere at—"

"Whoa, Tilley!" pleaded Bill. "The longer I talk to you, you dithering blithering optimist, the more certain it becomes that I must blow my brains out today, because of the certainty of death 60 years from today. Oh, I'll cover Old Twistibus Boulevard without event, by minding my own business, see? And by—but now I'm going to hang up. And I want you to ring me back—my expense, yes—the minute you unearth that pawn-ticket across the street and find out if the ring is redeemable."

"Consider it done," said Kirkaldy, "as soon as I can get across the street. Stay right where you are." And he hung up, as did Bill Chattock. Glad, the latter, to have learned at first hand some of the colourful details of the long twisting crawl in front of him, but not particularly perturbed about it. For the truck he was piloting was in perfect condition. There was plenty of gas in it, and then much to spare—in its special oversized tanks. There were two extra inner tubes inside the truck—two extra tyres. And a toolbox with every tool needed. And in which he'd even seen spare piston-rings, spark-plugs—whoever drove that truck regularly was an artist in carefulness.

So he held little dubitation that he'd be bowling down the Foleysburg-Spottsville Road toward dusk this evening, with safe and plenty margin to spare—as to fateful show-close. Bowling along, yes, to convey to Melody the thing she now least dreamed in the world could happen. That her father and mother *had* been married—by bell, book and candle.

But of course Bill Chattock could not know that Old Twistibus was a sinister, as well as a strange world, set off entirely as it was by man and geography from the world outside—a world, indeed, all its own; and that getting *into* it and *out* of it might be two different things.

CHAPTER XI

"PAW" ELUM

Bill, turning from the wall-phone, found that the topknotted, skinny, calico-clad Mrs. Elum had vanished—rather, had become transformed miraculously into a most weird caricature of herself. For what was in sight now, and coming forward, was only a skinny little elderly bald-headed man of about her exact build, clad in home-sewn trousers and shirt made of calico almost identical with what she wore, and with a short, square-cut grey beard. He was bent completely over double, so that his torso stood practically at right angles to his legs. Plainly, arthritis. He was in the act of skating, rather than walking, by means of sliding a short stool ever ahead of him toward the doorway, under one arm a crudely lettered pasteboard sign reading:

FRESH CAT TODAY, 2 cents a pound

Clear to the door he skated with his stool-crutch, hung his sign by two evidently bent-pin hooks protruding from it on the screen-wire inside. This accomplished, he brought forth from a hip pocket a huge corncob pipe which proved to be lighted all the time, for when he took a deep satisfying whiff from it, it filled the whole place with an odour composed seemingly of burning rubber and alfalfa.

It was plain, from the cautious fearful glance he threw around toward the bead-hung rear quarters with his little blue eyes, why he took position here at the door, for the direction of the breeze through the place, such as there was, was such as to carry the foul fumes out the screen.

Bill cleared his throat.

"I beg your pardon, but I'm—"

"Know all 'bout it, sarcus-driver," said the little old man, in a cackling voice almost like that of his wife. "Do all the phonin' ye want—and settle up a'tter yo're done. I'm Paw Elum. Maw tolt me 'bout you. She's laid down now to take her aft'noon siesta."

"Sies—hrmph—yes. Well, I'll stick around here, Mr. Elum, a few minutes, if you don't mind. Party I just called is going to—say, do you mind telling me—uh—ah—do you mind telling me—if people around here really eat cats?"

He felt a shiver in the pit of his stomach. "Do they eat—cat?" said the little old man, profoundly shocked. "W'y, shore they do. W'y wouldn't they? The fat 'un whut goes 'ficially on sale now is the fattest an' finest cat ever brung out'n th' Valley. Young'un what toted it in on his shoulder was afear'd to fetch it to me 'caze I'd threatened to whop the billy-hell out'n him ef'n I ever cotched him in here 'gain, the—the little cracker-stealin' varmint. So he t'uk it to Ced'ville Road, an' sold it fer 5 cents. They brung it here, an' sold it fer 10."

"Are—are there cats—roaming in the Valley?" asked Bill.

"Wa-all," said Paw thoughtfully, taking a good whiff on his rubbish kiln, "'pends on what you call roamin'. This 'un roamed too durned fur from Mud River, an' got himself cotched 'way up in Cat'mount Creek."

"Oh!" said Bill, relieved. For he liked cats. "A—a fish, eh?"

"Good Gordy," said Paw Elum, almost disgruntledly, "but you shore air a city man, ain't ye? Yep, I reckon catfish is the name I should'a' used. Catfish, yes. This 'un, what's layin' now in a tub o' spring water back in the woodshed, is all o' 20 pound. Whar you 'spectin' yore call from?"

"Wine City. Chap there is going to put my mind to rest about something, so I can get going. I'm going to have the charges reversed—and pay you the commission on both calls."

"Glory be!" said Paw Elum. "Looks like Maw an' me'll make a leetle money this day. We git moughty little trade 'cep'n a trickle by way o' the three roads what all come t'gether jest beyant the rise ahead o' ye."

"Well," comforted Bill, "you'll make some profit today. If, that is, I don't lope out—without paying!" He was but being facetious.

"Ef you did," said Paw quite frankly, but gravely, "Maw an' me'd be stuck plenty bad. 'Caze ef'n you loped out, an' I had to call the sher'ff to go in atter ye, caze ye didn't pay, he—he wouldn't do it. He's skeered as all git-out o' goin' in that thar Valley. Skeered he'll git a bullet f'm some clump o' und'brush."

Bill frowned.

"Bad actors down there, eh?" he ventured. Scratched his chin. "Maybe they'll take a pot-shot at me."

"No, no, no," deprecated Paw Elum promptly. "They hain't no feelin's 'ginst furr'ners. It's jest a puss'nel feud atween Jock Southey, the sherr'f, an' them, account him 'rresting one, an' gittin' him hanged, fer murderin' all three of his idjit daughters. Now he stays out'n thar. Says let 'em feud them-sevves out'n the way. Yep, they feud down thar, yep. No, he let's Willie-Willie be 'fficial messenger—'bout what goes on."

"Willie-Willie! That intrigues me. How did he ever get named that?"

"That's simple," said Paw. "I got all the facks f'm somebody down thar what knows all 'bout it, Seems 'at his maw an' paw, when alive, and him a new-borned baby, fit like cat'mounts 'bout who should name him. Trouble 'uz each wanted to name him Willie, on'y each wanted it to show 'at his or her word 'uz law in that cabin. So-o-o, they fin'lly named him Willie-Willie—'t'd prove each had gottened their own way."

Bill smiled broadly. "That's a life-time proof, all right. So he's the man in love with the lady novelist, eh?"

"Yes, the goof. Ef'n he don't take keer of his hontin' an' trappin' he'll plumb starve t' death this winter."

"Hunting and trapping, eh? My friend—the chap I had on the wire a while back, and who's been by here once himself—he says the people down in there are pretty benighted. Is that right?"

"Wa-all," deprecated Paw, "ain't never none of 'em as I've heered of b'en hit by the King on the shoulder, an' named 'Sir.' The real fack is that they air livin' in intellectyal darkyness. Don't know, most of 'em, that this is the 19th Century."

"Nineteen—ah—um—yes—well, they see planes passing over 'em and all that, don't they?"

"Mister, ef you look at a a'rmail or a'r-route map o' this kentry, you'll see 'at not one line goes over this hyar region. Me, I've seed planes up overhead when Maw and me lived in Swampville. And Maw she's even sot in one, for a minute, on a field jest out'n Price-town. No, the people in that there Valley don't b'lieve—many of 'em an'way—a man kin fly."

"Don't believe—but what do they think of the things they hear on their radios—even more—what about the soldiers of them, who came back from the war and told them all the amazing stories of combat in the air and—"

"Mister, ain't ye never heerd o' the liter'cy tests? Wasn't but 5 in the whole Valley who passed it. And them 5—wa-al, one come walkin' out hyar a y'ar ago, with his few things in a bundle on his shoulder. On'y one what ever went back at all. I'd seed him a while here when he went gaily in—to-tin' a leetle batt'ry raddio fer his folks. I ast him, w'en he come out, how they liked the raddio—and he said—he said his paw busted it to pieces 'ith a saplin' th' minute it started to squawk—them voices 'uz sperrits, he said his paw said—condemned sperrits in hell, else they wouldn't be in no box, an' ef'n a man listened to 'em he'd burn in hell fer a mill'on y'ars. An' when I ast this returned sojer w'y in tarnation he wasn't stayin', he said 'A butt'fly caint nev' become a cat'pillar ag'in.'"

"That was putting it pretty aptly," commented Bill. "It—but this Willie-Willie—whose maternal and paternal progenitors fought like catamounts? Has he another name?"

"Oh, shore. Noon. Name's Willie-Willie Noon."

"Noon! Noon? Not related—by any chance—is he, to Mr. Hickory Noon, banker, back in Pricet—"

"The same," nodded Paw. "Him an' Hick 'uz left, as boys, with their maw w'en their paw died, chawed t' death by a cat'mount. And she couldn't raise both. So a cousin t' Pricetown he said he'd take one boy. Well, Hick'ry, he wanted to go to the Big Town—the bright lights, see? An' Willie-Willie he wanted to stay with his maw. He did, and Hick'ry did. And now Hick'ry's pres'dent of a bank, and all."

"Proving, therefore, the theory of euthenics instead of eugenics?"

"Yo're ovah m' haid, mister. Way over. I—but listen, mister. Yo're havin' to lose a heap of time, ain't ye, waitin' a call f'm outside? Maw says you gotta be in Foleysburg t'night?"

"That's right. But I'll step on the gas when I get out of—"

"You won't step on no gas down thar," said Paw. "Else you'll find yorese'f in a clomp o' bushes. But here! I don't know but what I kin put you to a way o' making up *all* the time yo're losin' hyar."

"You—can? How, I'd like to know?"

"Wa-all, I see Willie-Willie, this mo'nin', 'arly, ridin' 'ith one of the drivers of one of the trock an' trailer trains. Showin' he'd b'en to Pricetown to see the sarcus, or else his brother, or both. Now he mought have b'en brung home by Mist' MacWhorter as a favour—but he mought, too, to've fin'lly put down that thar vehicle bridge he 'uz alluz talkin' 'bout—over Cat'mount Creek, a leetle ways from th' leetle wayfarer bridge—by fellin' a couple o' huge trees acrost and layin' planks. W'ich, ef he did, 'd save any veh'cle f'm havin' to go down the creek one side to the reg'lar bridge, and all the way back on t'other. It's called, that p't'c'lar traipse, ha'r-pin bend. And's a full hour's drive. Now ef Willie-Willie was a-guidin' Mist' Mac-Whorter to this new bridge—"

"Sounds good—but how in heaven's name can I find Willie-Willie to find out where his new bridge might be? I—"

"Yo' won't need to. Jest you call Miss Crestfield, the lady nov'list. Twirl the crank four times. Four times on'y, see? The road it forks two ways bey-ant her place. Ef'n she tells you the show it went right'ard this mornin' 'stid o' lef'ard then Willie-Willie was a-guidin' Mist' Mac. But ef now it went left'ard, then Willie-Willie was jest a-bein' fetched home, and—"

"I'll—I'll call her now—before my long-distance call starts coming through, and get the low-down. Thanks a million. I—"

"Don't thank me, mister, 'twell you git her! She gall'vants 'round a lot, on a ol' bike what she's got, gittin' local colour fer her book. Ef'n a hillbilly-like voice answers the phone, it's Willie-Willie, moonin' 'round at her place, waitin' fer her return."

"Willie-Willie—*or* Saxone Crestfield," Bill said, turning about to the phone. "Either one will do, if they save me one little hour toward getting to Foleysburg. Yes, either one will do." He seized the crank protruding from the phone. "So here goes. One—two—three—four…"

Which identical words, oddly enough, were being sardonically uttered at this very moment in a trailer on the "lot" at Foleysburg by Jules DiValo, Demon Illusionist, to a strange little creature, seemingly half boy, half animal, that he had surreptitiously brought out of Idiot's Valley, as part of an ingenious, cunning and perfect scheme which would insure that William Chattock, due to start into that selfsame valley about noon this day, and be out by sundown or thereabouts, would *not* be out of there before tomorrow's sundown. And that his strange mission away from the show would be known—at least to one Melody Ashbrooke!—to be 101 per cent a failure. After all of which—nothing would matter. Since by tomorrow's sundown, Jules DiValo and Melody Ashbrooke, temporary residents of Topeka, Kansas, would be legally Mr. and Mrs. Jules DiValo.

Outside, DiValo could hear the usual unmistakable sounds of the Big Top going up—or at least the unmistakable signal cries and orders—under the expert management of Big Top Charley; and so knew that the show would open on the dot tonight as expected, But he continued to regard the sleeping boy who had failed to awaken at the sound of DiValo's measured counting.

The boy, about 11 years of age, was a hillbilly boy of the most extreme type. He was clad in a pair of ragged overalls, tattered at the bottom edges, one leg even shorter than the other, and the whole pair so faded by the hot suns of Old Twistibus Valley that they bespoke not only that they were hand-me-downs from an older brother, but that the older brother had, in turn, gotten them from an older brother yet! He was without shoes, but had a hat, of sorts, lying on the straw beside him: a hole-ridden sombrero with ragged, jagged brim. His long yellow hair was unkempt, matted, his face was speckled with thousands of freckles—and with his protuberant buck teeth that seemed to draw slightly in and out from his lips with each unconscious inspiration, he seemed to be one who had adenoids.

But like all hill folk—swamp folk—or even mountaineer folk!—naturally alert in the presence of something threatening, he must have felt DiValo's sour, almost malevolent gaze upon him, where he had heard quite nothing couched in the latter's familiar tones—for the boy sat suddenly and alarmedly up, rubbed freckled fists into blue eyes, and returned DiValo's gaze blinkingly.

"Be—be we thar, yit, Miste Devilo?"

"Hell-fire, you little oaf—ah—kid, we're there an hour ago," said DiValo unsmilingly. He had risen, as he had been speaking, from the bunk edge, to wrap his hastily-assumed dressing-gown about himself in reversed direction, revealing in the so doing that he was dressed beneath in neat grey-flannel trousers carelessly belted in to a cool open-throated white silk shirt, and in full keeping with the sockless ankles that rose from the comfortable white tennis shoes on his well-shaped feet. Now, wrapped in proper direction, so to speak, he was down on the bunk edge again. Was talking again. But suavely friendlily now. "The Big Top's even going up. And most of the outfit, I daresay—now that the trailer motion's let up—are about to catch some of that shut-eye that you've been having for the last few hours."

"But me, I hain't slep' all las' night nor night afore—'caount o' waitin' up fer to see the sarcus come th'ough Ol' Twistibus."

"Well—we came through all right, didn't we? And even stopped right in front of your place, at Halfway Point—isn't that the name?—for practically a half-hour? While we had machine inspection, and filled up some of the gas tanks from the gas-tank car, for the other and remaining half of that awful trek." DiValo continued to regard the boy studiedly. "Well, now—let's see—our name is—"

"Tobe Huck. 'Lijah Huck's littlest."

"'Lijah Huck! Your old man *would* be named Elijah all right. Well, now, see here, do you know why you're here—in this trailer—rather, this sardine-can on wheels!—with me?"

"'Co'se do! Hit's 'caze Paw, when he ast you, back thar, what you done in the sarcus, an' you tolt him you did a mag'can ack, ast ef'n you couldn't use a right-smart boy in it to he'p you. Fer me, I *kin* do magick—even ef'n, mister, you didn't ast me to show you nothin' befur you tu'k me on—look—"

He took a chipped marble out of the tattered pocket of his faded blue shirt, and with it made the simplest of false passes, in which he held it lightly between his left thumbtip and index fingertip, seized it apparently with the other hand—except that, of course, he dropped it into the holding hand!—and then followed the false clenched fist inexorably with his eye.

"Not bad—not bad!" said DiValo ungrudgingly, willing, as an artist, to acknowledge a shade of artistic ability in any other! And furthermore admitting to himself alone that the boy had mastered the hardest feature of all, in the false passes: the not looking at the hand which held the object. "But watch *me,* now—with this 50-cent piece."

And with the coin, which he had to extract from a trousers pocket under the dressing-gown, he made the expert false pass, wiping it apparently from the fingertips of his right hand on to the palm of his left, except, of course, that in the transit of his right hand to his left, he had deftly swung the coin, by his fingertips, into the palm of the hand that carried it, and thus, with his left, carried off a fistful of emptiness.

Which, with a light tossing gesture, he revealed to be pure emptiness—except that the gesture, even to his own eye, gave the striking illusion that a coin flew up in the air—and vanished in mid-air; and then, looking reflectively first at one shoetip, and then the other, he leaned over to the left one and "drew" the half-dollar right out of it, by pushing the coin downward back of his extended right fingers with the thumb of the hand that held it, so that it appeared to slide right out of the shoe leather. A striking illusion, DiValo knew, even at the 5 or 6 feet that separated him from his present rapt audience.

"Jee—hunkus!" the boy breathed. "'At's slick. Diff'ent 'n mine. How do yu—"

"Thus," sighed DiValo. And demonstrated the *modus operandi*—in slow motion—and with the edge of his "passing" hand, including the back thereof, toward his lone audience.

"Jee—hunkus!" said the boy again. "Shore wisht I had me a fo'-bit piece—shor'd practise that 'un."

"Hell-fire, kid, your mitt won't be big enough to palm a half-dollar in it, like I just did, for 10 years yet. But first: I want to know if you know the arrangements by which you're here—with me—as my assistant—to even sort of learn my act, so to speak."

"An'—an' to someday, mebbe," put in the boy eagerly, "in y'ars an' y'ars, take over yore ack—when yo've got rich in it."

DiValo's lip curled in a bitter sneer.

"Take it over—yeah," he said sardonically. "As I did. By the way, boy, where on earth did you ever get hold of the word 'act' for just what it is I do here with this show? And, moreover, the word 'magic'?"

"Whar? W'y 'caze Mist' MacWhorter, w'en I 'uz a leetle boy, an' the show hi't got stuck one day nigh us—got stuck jest off'n Jeb Dollar's place for three—four—hour—'caze a driver he got pendenitis an' some old clown what was a doc oncet hadda cut him open in Jeb's cabin and taken his pendicum out—"

"Yes, our Karl the Klown. One of the greatest of his day, once, in medicine and surgery. Now a booze-nose. Yes, I've heard about that time. MacWhorter's all kinds of a soft-hearted old fool. Could have gone on that day, but no—had to find out fully how his man came out. Now if he ran this show of his right, instead of letting in a lot of brats free every night, and—go ahead?"

"Wa-a-all, 'at's all. W'ile the show h'it 'uz stuck thar, he had some th' p'fawmers put on some acks fer we-'uns all. He called 'em acks. One them acks was mag'cal, he said. Oh, it 'uz won'rful. A man he et a kyard—"

"Kyard?"

"Yeah, a kyard out'n a deck. He et it."

"Oh, yes, I know. Tissue-paper overlay overlying a paper-thin card-sized biscuit. Go ahead?"

"An'—an' he shot at a—a board 'ith a gun, an' the kyard it come out'n his stommick an' stuck t' th' board."

"Pah!" said DiValo. "He certainly ladled 'you-'uns' the poorest he had. But here, damn it, I asked you a question. Do you know the arrangements under which you're here?"

The boy blinked oddly. "No."

"Damn you! "DiValo bit out. "You know something. You—listen here, where the hell were you when I stepped back to that corncrib of your old man's and talked certain things over with him?"

"I wuz on my belly onder the crib, lookin' at it, w'en you an' Paw come in. An' I—I cain't he'p it ef you don't b'lieve me."

"Oh, I *do* believe you. Implicitly. Now that I've got you on your belly under that crib! All right. And so there, on your belly, you caught a couple of earfuls of a business dicker, didn't you? Well come on now, what did you hear? Tell me now? So what did you hear there? Come on now, you young ra—er— Tobe," DiValo corrected himself craftily, "what did you hear?"

"Wa-all," returned the boy reluctantly, "I heer'd you an' Paw make a dicker 'at w'en a white trock 'ith letters on h'it spellin' the same like thing as whut's on the sarcus trocks—a w'ite trock driv' by a man in purply pants an' a grey hat on his head, come th'ough Ol' Twistibus in fi—six—hour, Paw 'uz to—to—"

"—to delay him? Worse—hamstring his further progress by—is that what you're trying to tell me?"

"Don' know nothin' 'bout no ham," said the boy sullenly. "But—but Paw he showed you—showed how—how he could easy do—whut you wanted. Which 'uz to—to holt the man thar in th' Valley. To—to holt him thar."

"I guess you heard direct all right. Well, *what* did you hear directly?"

"W'y Paw—Paw says as how he—he'll step out inter th' road an' flag the man—an'—an' ast him ef he could fotch a pore old man with a brokened hip to his brother's—on the Foleysburg Road. Brother whut's—whut's a doc. Paw—Paw 'uz to say the old man gonna die ef'n he hain't gotten thar t'day."

"We-ell, you heard all right, all right. And when this purpled-pantied chappie climbed down off his truck and went back along the path to your cabin to at least look the poor old injured man over—"

"Gran'pappy!" cried Tobe delightedly. "Oh, Gran'pappy 'uz to lay an' groan like. Gran'pappy he do an'thing fer a little chaw-t'baccy. He 'uz to—to lay and groan like. An'—an' then Hank—he's the next 'un 'bove me—Hank 'uz t' sneak up outside, and drap the saplin' pole atween th' cleats whut's hidden ahin' the vines. An' jim the door tight, jest like h'it's t' be jimmed ef'n ever the Cadwalladers they git inside, an' we-'uns air on the outside, an' then we kin burn 'em up—

"Ne' mind the technique of trapping people in feuds. And burning 'em alive—woof! Tell me what was to happen after Master Hank quietly dropped the trap-bar across the door? How was your father to explain to the stranger about this so-unfortunate occurrence?"

"Oh, I know whut you mean. Paw he 'uz to say one o' the young-'uns—the damned young-'uns f'm up-road—'uz up to they tricks ag'in. An' to jest set a spell twell 'nother one he comes 'long, an' he gits him t' raise the bar."

Jules DiValo nodded noncommittally. "And while the stranger fumes and figures, and Gran'pappy no doubt gets properly sceptical about going away from home and kinfoik—what?"

"Oh, m' brother Bump—he's the big 'un of us all—Bump, he 'uz t' be all th' w'ile in a clomp o' bushes t'other side th' road, with his b'ar rifle—an' Bump is to fire all the bullets in that b'ar rifle into this here man's gas-tank—Bump he knows whar 'tis 'caount o' workin' a week in a garagy at Fox Crossin' outside th' Valley—them thar bullets is steel-tipped—oh, they'll kill a b'ar or a—wa-all, Bump's to pump 'em all into the gas-tank, an'—an' let the gas run out'n the tank on to th' graound."

"A thing which," mused Jules DiValo, "with half a dozen gaping holes actually torn in the metal, will take five minutes—no more. And I suppose—but do you know what your Paw was to say—when this shoot-fest commences?"

"Oh, he 'uz to say 'somebody shootin' at a b'ar. Hope he gits him!'"

"Which may or may not make the guest feel more at ease," nodded Jules sardonically. "But giving 4 or 5 minutes, according to the laws of Physics, for the gas to all run out—just how far, youngster, will this leave Mr. Man—from Civilization?"

"Wa-all, on'y thutty mile mebbe as crow flies—but seven'y mile, mo' o' less, by foot."

"Well, now for the—the fireworks. I mean," DiValo prompted gently, "after Gran'pappy finally refuses to be moved at all from kith, kindred, home and castle—as per arrangement pre-made with your paw!—and the lock-bar gets raised again by Hank, posing as a gentle-natured young-'un from up road—and the man and Paw get outside—what is to be told the man as to how it happens that all that thar b'ar-shootin' outside has resulted—in his being gasless?"

"W'y," said Tobe, "Paw's to sw'ar that the Cadwalladers whut he b'en feudin' with for twenty year done that shootin and drawin' off o' that gas—out'n spite 'ginst an'body what'd even go in our place an' have truck with us. But he tolt you, you know, how he'd tell the stranger that a gas an' ile wagon'd be th'ough Ol' Twistibus next day sometime—at least far's Half-way P'int—whut could sell him mo' gas—and that them thar holes could easy be plugged up 'ith some lead from some melted bullets—Paw 'uz even to say he'd he'p the stranger to plug 'em—an' so, 'caount all this, the stranger'd hafta put up 'ith us fer the night—that is, ef'n he didn't 'ject to percabbage an' streaker meat fer vittles."

"Not that," said DiValo gently, "that a gas wagon *would* be through—next day?"

"Lordy no!" exclaimed Tobe. "Gas wagon don't come on'y evvy few months. 'Twon't be th'ough fer 'nother few weeks yit, I reckon. Maybe months. Fer hain't none o' us no whar's down yit to borrowin' coal ile from each other—like we alluz air 'bout 3 weeks afore the ile wagon comes. *An'* fer that thar feller not gittin' out o' the Valley t'day, ner prob'ly t'morrow nuther, you 'greed, to Paw, Mister Devilo, to take me on as 'sstant."

"Now wait. You wouldn't hold out on your Uncle Jules, would you? Didn't you get the—er—rationale of my believing said individual should not get back to the show today, and, in great probability, tomorrow either?"

Tobe's face was a pitiful blankness. "The low-down," DiValo explained, "of my feeling why he should not get back?"

"Oh, y'as—y'as. I know whut ye mean now. W'y, you tolt Paw he 'uz a man who was marrit to a 'ooman a'ready but 'uz fig'ahin' to marry 'ith a gal in th' sarcus. An' you an' th' others an' Mist' MacWhorter wanted to save that gal. An' then I seen ye give Paw $10, an' heered you say 'at ef'n that man didn't git back to the show today, I 'uz to stay on with you fer y'ars—an' l'arn yore ack—an' 'at, 'sides, you'd mail Paw 'nother $15. Care Elums, outside th' Valley. Whar Paw he said he could git a letter by somebody comin' th'ough by mewlback. An' so he'p me, Mister Devilo, that's all I heered."

"Well, Tobe, think your father 'll—er—hold that man back successfully in the valley?"

"Think?" echoed Tobe. "Jup'ter Priest, Mister Devilo, yo' don't 'pear to know whut 15 dollars 'll do 'round our place! W'y we-'uns kin buy store stuff fer 6 months on $15. Mister Devilo, they ain't no more chanct o' that thar man gittin' out'n th' Valley t'day, oncet he goes an' takes a look at Gran'pappy, than they is of—wa-all, of Paw an' Eb Cadwallader settin' down t'gether t' a dish o' co'n pone an' 'lasses."

"I see," nodded DiValo. "It seems that you know a lot. More, perhaps, than is good for you. But as my—er—valued assistant, it is best that we have no secrets from each other. But now I have to ask *you* a question. And here it is: Do you know about the new law in America? The new law, I mean, just passed by Congress? The law, I mean, that anybody who drains—or causes to be drained—get that, now!—the gas out of the tank of a vehicle that is more than 40 miles from a town, hangs."

"Hangs?" The boy went pale. His knees slipped from his fingers. His freckles became momentary discs of black against the whiteness of his face. "Bump—hang?—"

"Aw, keep your shirt on. Nobody need ever know. Who knows, as it is? I do. You do. Your father does. And Brother Bump, say. But with your father and Bump keeping their mouths shut, as they assuredly will—for I cautioned your father about the new law!—and me naturally never telling anybody so long as *I* live, lest they spill it—certainly *you'll* never blab, since—"

"Me—blab?" repeated Tobe, aghast. "Hell, no! I'll—I'll never tell. I—I don't want to hang."

"Then just keep your trap shut as long as you live about how that gas got drained out on Old Twistibus. Make all that your life secret, Tobe."

DiValo stood up; feeling down in his trousers pocket again, inside his crimson dressing-gown, he withdrew two coins—both quarters—and examining not the faces at all, but the edges, kept the one which, though smoother, was more strongly milled—which could, therefore, be held in a palm. "Watch this now," he commanded. And twice, slowly, repeated that same expert pass he had made a while back. Then tossed the coin to the boy seated on the straw. "Now you practise this pass for a half-hour. While I run outside and make a couple of calls to some other performers in this outfit. See how adept you can become on this one pass."

"Yessir, I shore will." The boy, quarter in fingers, looked respectfully at his new master. "How soon, Mister Devilo, do you reckon 'twill be befur I kin do yore ack?"

"D*o* my act?" retorted DiValo sardonically. "Hell fire, young bozo, you'll not only—now you just keep *this* under your hat, now, with certain matters appertaining to hangings and gasolene—but, if certain things work out now as I think they will—from the time this show leaves Foleysburg, you'll not only have to do the act—but, sir, you'll even have to *be* the act!"

"Be—th'—ack?" gasped Tobe, turning pale again. "Wen th'—th' show leaves Fole'sburg?"

"And why not?" purred DiValo. "Doesn't the famous old adage run: The Show Must Go On? And with the Illustrious DiValo hotfooting it westward, in company with the sweetest and prettiest thing this lousy outfit contains, who else should carry on the gr-r-reat act but Tobe, the Demon Illusionist, whose pappy—and his pappy's stalwart sons, and b'ar rifles, and trappin' bars, and a decoy consisting of one lively hippity-hoppity old Methuselah—put this whole thing right in the bag? Yowsah!"

The boy, seated against the wall, was clumsily, but fascinatedly, essaying the pass. DiValo turned to the trailer door.

"In case anybody comes in the next ten minutes, and has to see me, tell 'em you're my new assistant, and that I'm over talking to Harry the Living Skeleton. And," he added, "if anyone comes in later than ten minutes from now, tell 'em I'm talking with Melody, the Spot Girl. Or can't you remember—even those names?"

"Harry 'r Mel'dy," rumbled the boy. "Harry 'r Mel'dy."

"Good enough," said DiValo. "I don't think anybody will come buzzing around, however. All right, I'm off. Watch your step-ins!"

With which, opening the trailer door, he stepped down into the "lot," closing the trailer door expertly behind him as he did so.

The "lot" was still in considerable confusion. Garish red and gilt panel-covered "wagons" stood about, pointed in various directions, and some of the heavier ones had made deep ruts in the loamlike black dirt. Off a distance from all the vehicles, and trailers too—and resplendent in silver gilt and bright scarlet, the scarlet spelling danger from lights!—and guarded, even now, by a worker, was the tank car which always travelled along, and protected the gas supply for the whole procession.

Further beyond the area where all this parking had taken place, the Big Top was going up—had gone up, did one judge from the still somewhat irregular mass of brown canvas now magically standing off ground, and DiValo could hear, within it, the sound of knockdown seats being hastily knocked together. And rented second-hand planks being laid.

And now a sneering, triumphant satisfaction filled DiValo's soul as his gaze fell upon that smaller "tent" that was right now being erected off to one side of the big tent—the tent which tonight would house him and his activities for the last time. Now he had reached the opposite line of trailers—had reached the safety of the midmost one, in fact, and was turning down it, with a momentary uneasy glance back over his shoulder to where a great snake of a trunk rose gently and undulatingly above a 10-foot-high canvas "wrap wall"—a wrap-wall being, of course, nothing but a great ribbon of canvas hung loosely about 4 pointed poles jabbed into the earth.

"I hope that damned behemoth's tethered in there safely to his stake," he said. "For you never can tell when that other human behemoth that owns him—Big Dolly—may unhook him because the chain hurts Babykin's tootsie!" He shook his head. "Too much animal coddling around here. Mac-Whorter, secretly feeding his own steak on steak-nights to Princess! Just because when she got out that time, she went to sleep in a chicken house, and never touched a fowl." But now DiValo was going down the line of trailers, except that he had to stop abruptly as a woman climbed hurriedly down out of the entrance of an orange-and-blue one directly in front of him. She was a woman of close on to 40, light in build, and muscular in swing, and with peroxided hair in nickel-plated curlers so that it stuck oddly up from her head like the hair on a Circassian beauty. She was none other than Princess Zaida, High-Wire Expert—even if on the books of the show she was set down as Virlyn Mongoven. Determination was written strongly on her face, and DiValo knew that she was on her way with her daily complaint to MacWhorter, patiently listening to all such at each point of arrival.

She stopped, as had DiValo. Automatically—even coquettishly—she adjusted her curled hair. For she liked him, and he knew she liked him!

"Hi, Card-Riffler," she said, "hear what Baron Munchausen's latest is?"

"No, what?" he replied. For the driver, known as Baron Munchausen, was invariably digging up a new one.

"He brought it back," she laughed, "from Idiot's Valley. Drove the last trailer through today—"

He stiffened.

"Baron—Baron—drove the last trai—I thought Truthful Tom always wound up the procession?"

"Oh," she explained, "they exchanged driver's seats this morning for a while. For luck, I guess. No, Baron was last. At least on the stretch where he claims this one happened! So he can't be confuted, see? It is that a pretty woman in the east end of the Valley stopped him—asked him if her husband, William Chattock, was with this outfit."

DiValo stood in disgruntled silence. Then asked:

"Did—did he tell this to—to Melo—to the Ashbrooke girl? She—she kind of likes the chap a little."

"Oh, yes," Princess Zaida said. "Told all the women in the outfit who might be interested. After we pulled in here, that is. Fact is, I was in Melody's trailer with her and Big Dolly when he knocked—and rendered."

"What—what did Melo—the Ashbrooke girl say?"

Princess Zaida shook her head as one in mental communion with some other deprecating shake of the head she was evidently thinking of. "She said what neither Dolly nor I could frame into words—she said "Pathetic, isn't it, how poor Baron Munchausen is running out of ideas? There was a time, even when I came on here, that he'd at least have invented a dinosaur—splashing about in that swamp at the west end of that valley!'"

He nodded silently. "Yes, there was," was all he could say.

"Well, I'm off," she said. "To see if I can't get Mr. Mac to have Princess fed before I do my act each night. She rumbled last night for her chow right when I was on the wire, and—well I'm off."

And off she was, and off he was, too, renewing his journey. But saying to himself in sheer utter disgust of soul:

"My stars—can you beat it? After that obliging piece of femininity back in the Valley helped out my little 'rib,' it had to be Baron Munchausen—who was to carry it on through—instead of Truthful Tom! Now if only Tom had brought that little story back—if only Tom—but, oh well. It doesn't particularly change the set-up one bit. Not at all!"

He reached a gorgeous purple trailer with horizontal orange stripes, and through a half-open window in it he called loudly:

"Hi, Harry—you in there?"

"Come in—come in," called a thin voice.

DiValo opened the door and stepped up in. This was the trailer for the tent crew. But one man was in it just now; he sat on the edge of his bunk, under the light from the very window through which DiValo had called, mending, with needle and thread, a white cotton undershirt. A pair of black pants, hanging from the edge of the bunk, showed where another mending job had just been crudely completed.

He was thinner, this man, than even a sliver from the proverbial rail! The head that looked up, momentarily, was like a skull covered with parchment. "I see you're alone, Harry," DiValo said, to the Living Skeleton.

"Right," grunted the other, squinting down at his needling again. "Advantage of riding in the tent-crew trailer. I get a chance to sleep—*when I* get there!"

"Yeah?" returned DiValo, drawing out from under a nearby bunk a single small wooden stool. He dropped down on it. "But you're not sleeping now? Say, Harry, I've a question I want to ask you. A question about Bill Chattock. Rather his—er—psyche!"

"Psyche is good!" grunted the other. "An old word of mine own, even! Well, now that two gentlemen with vocabularies hold discussion, I'll so much as correct you and say you are undoubtedly asking something about Bill Chattock's psychology."

"His psychology? Well, I said his psyche."

"Yes, but psyche has a metaphysical aspect to it."

"All right!—his psychology?"

"Shoot," returned the other imperturbably, punching his needle through the cloth. "I guess, having been in the outfit with him now for quite a good while, I know Bill Chattock's general slant as well as he does himself. He's one not easily shaken from a trail he follows—as long as there's the slightest chance to upturn something."

"Please!" pleaded DiValo. "Don't rehearse things about Bill Chattock that I know as well as I know my—10 toes! What in your estimation would Bill Chattock do—er—have done if, for instance, he'd had a small accident today along Old Twistibus—to his truck, I mean, not himself. Like—well, like, say, stripping a gear. And no gear to substitute. What I mean is: would he have stayed with that truck, in your estimation, or would he have attempted to leg it out to Civilization afoot?"

"You have the confoundedest way of mis-using tenses, DiValo," complained the Living Skeleton. "Bill Chattock would stick with the truck, come hell or high heaven. Because it's Mr. Mac's property. And because it always has a couple of hundred dollars in its concealed safe, for change for the next show. Oh, he might ask somebody going through there to phone in here, once out of that Valley, to MacWhorter, and have a car come—but whoa, Tilley!—I forgot about this crazy town with the title to every foot of land in it—and the county, to boot—tied up by the provisions of no electric wiring to be in, on, or over it—and hence no phones!—well, he'd just stay with the truck till finally, not catching up by, say, Spottsville, MacWhorter decided to send a runner-car back along the route for general good measure. Answered?"

"Yes. Yes. And what you narrate is exactly what I think."

"That's what *you* thought?" The Living Skeleton's eyes burned into DiValo's. "Well, why the hell did you ask me for, then?"

"Oh, the fellow interests me, that's all. Harry, I'm going to have to ask you to do me a favour—a small one—I don't like to ask it—but ask it I *must*—and *rendered* it must be."

"You don't have to be so apologetic about asking a favour. Shoot! It must be an odd one—that you close the window there to the world outside. So what is it?"

"I'm going to have to ask you to confirm—or corroborate—as happening to yourself—a small incident that happened to *me* this morning. To confirm it, that is, to Melody. For if *I* tell her—and it's for her own good that she be told, you see—she'll have all the reason in the world to suspect the information at the source, and hence—"

"Already," said Harry sagely, stopping his sewing for a few minutes, "I can see the structure of some kind of a legerdemain trick—rising through the fog! Something, I glean, in the sphere of—expert lying. In short, I sense that you want some utter damned lie bolstered up. Well, my hearty, much as I get along with you, because you are a man of intellect like myself, I won't depart from my veracity standard around this outfit—much less to that girl—orphan as she is."

"What I want you to do for me is to confirm a certain episode—confirm it, only as happening to you—not to me."

"Hold ever'thing," said Harry dryly. "Like the horse who went to the tank, I will only say I don't know nothin' 'bout nothin'. For anything I might confirm as happening to me—when it didn't—could be one whopping, damned lie. And that is O—U—T, out. And so the answer to your petition is—in advance—no."

"I see," half-laughed DiValo again. "No help, eh, from my old sidekick just one spot next mine on the platform? Well, well, well? And so I suppose

I shall just have to become, here and now, a little tough. Say, Harry, when do you and Meta, the Human Dumpling, expect to be in the same outfit again?"

The Living Skeleton's face grew hungry—of a man who was lonely, desperately lonely, for someone he loved. "Just as soon, DiValo, as either she and I can get in an outfit together as Skeleton *and* Fat Woman or, conversely, when Big Dolly on this trick gets hooked up to an outfit that can pay more rental for her elephant."

"Complicated, isn't it?" mused DiValo. "Like checkers! We have to move a fat woman off a square, to move another one on—and thus make them all happy with their husbands—or their elephants! Well, it oughtn't be long now."

"Thank God it won't," breathed the Skeleton.

"But that brings me back," persisted DiValo sadly, "to my platform pal's unwillingness to do a small—such a small!—favour for me. And which, as I started to say, back there, makes it necessary now for me to tell the authorities—of a certain State—that one 'Harry Kiskowicz,' of the Mac-Whorter Shows, is married, to Meta, a fat lady, when he already has a wife, even though somewhat rangy, in the State of—or," DiValo broke off, with assumed naiveness, "are the laws of bigamy different, Harry, for Living Skeletons?"

The Living Skeleton had been sitting, over the course of DiValo's last 30 words, with his lantern-jaw open, and needle poised grotesquely in mid-air.

"Well—what are you going to do? Is it money? If so, Meta will dig. How much—"

"Money? My—dear—Harry! DiValo the Demon Illusionist doesn't want money. I want you merely to narrate, to a 101 per cent degree of convincingness, and as happening to yourself, a small curious incident that happened to *me* this morning—really it did, Harry, though I can't prove it—to narrate this *for* and *to* Melody—and remember, it's all for her own good, see?—all for her own good, yes!—and to see to it, furthermore, that your—ah—establishment of this incident, in the particular manner described, as a bona fide incident happening to yourself, remains a 100 per cent inviolable secret between you and me."

"If you go too far in what you ask me to do, DiValo, I'll—I'll show you the spirit of a Living Skeleton in a way you'll never forget." His words trailed wearily away as those of a man who feared he was only speaking words—not meaning them. "What—what is it you want?" he almost wailed.

"All that you will do in this case, Harry," DiValo said firmly, and gently, "will be to bring conclusively about a marriage between Melody Ashbrooke, a white girl, and Jules DiValo, a white man—and very much so, as you can see for yourself! And what I mean by that, Harry, is that—and this is where I must violate a great secret known to but three persons alone—what I mean by my words, Harry, is that Bill Chattock—the man Melody Ashbrooke might have married—is **1**/16th Negro. Now do you feel better?" Harry opened cavernous eyes, which showed extreme horror—disgust.

"Bill—a nigger?" he said. "Oh, come, come, DiValo—that doesn't sound credible. What are you driving at?"

"That," pronounced DiValo coolly, "is why he so mysteriously left the outfit—a week ago. It was to dig up proof—at least of a sort!—that he wasn't, see? Melody, who I'll admit to you had been sort of oscillating between him and myself, said she'd give him till show-close tonight. Oh, it was merely a matter of unearthing the records of a certain white-to-white marriage back in his ancestry. Anyway, ask her if he didn't leave the outfit to investigate the possibility of the existence of a certain marriage—or, marriage record. And if she tells you yes, then you'll know, won't you, that all I'm telling you now is on the level?"

"All right, all right," said Harry. "But suppose," he now asked, "that when Chattock gets here today, with that truck, he has the proof—how do you know he won't have the proof he went after?"

"Chattock," said DiValo firmly, "isn't trailing us today. He's not coming through Old Twistibus. Doesn't even know anything, so far as that goes, about the commission he's supposed to have received. He never even came to Pricetown. Never—"

"Well—uh—ah—I don't *know* you know this—but we should go and tell MacWhorter at once—if, that is, we can prove it—"

"Quiet, you skin-stretched fool," said DiValo harshly. "If you value your own personal affairs being kept quiet, you'll pipe down on what I tell you. Even as to MacWhorter."

"I give up. All right. Mr. Mac won't worry about his office truck until pull-out time tomorrow. Now how do you know that Chattock's not on his way here—out of Old Twistibus?"

"How? I'll tell you how. Harry, this morning when we threaded out of Simpson's Junction, at the end of Idiot's Valley, I got out and took myself a little gander back in those woods along there to pick myself a wild flower or two—well, I heard a low whistle toward me, from back in the woods. So I threaded in past and there, in a little clearing, who do you think I came on?"

"Bill Chattock, of course," said the Skeleton sepulchrally.

"Oh, don't be so sceptical," warned DiValo. "Because that's exactly who it was."

"Of course," said Harry dryly. "And he explained his ability to have been there—instead of in Pricetown—or in Old Twistibus, or what have you?"

"Of course," said DiValo blandly. "He told me, in fact, that he never got any detailed letter of instruction from MacWhorter. Or sent any confirming telegram. For the very simple reason that he decided suddenly, there in Detroit, where he'd just written to Mac, to call it a day—yes, he admitted sadly to me there that he hadn't been able to disprove his Negro blood and so he was calling it—a day, see? But just couldn't face Melody. No! So wasn't even going to rejoin the show. But he did want her told at Foleysburg, and on the q.t., that he hadn't established that 'certain marriage'—so that she would be free to take the step she implied that she would be taking. And I now ask you, Harry; would Melody ever believe that story if *I* told it to her?"

"Hell, no!" said Harry. "For I don't even believe it myself. That is, I—I don't say I do or that I don't. If you told this story to Melody, she might be—ah—convinced perhaps that you'd laid a trap in Old Twistibus to delay Chattock."

"What kind of a trap could I have laid for anyone in Old Twistibus?"

"Don't be naive, DiValo," snapped Harry. "A little money would go a long way down there—and you know it. A huge felled tree—rolled by a family of those half-wits across the road—and then a 'strike called' when it came to rolling it back! Or the planks removed from that plank bridge we rolled over at some creek beyond Halfway Point, and hidden. That's the sort of thing Melody *might* suspect if *you* told her this true—even if true—tale. And so she'd give Chattock a break by at least waiting on for his 'proof' so far as Spottsville—then perhaps Cactus Cross Roads—then Hootens Falls—then—well, she just never would leave the show with you. For that, I take it, is what she's promised to do."

"Yes." And DiValo now knew that sales value a-plenty lay in that word, with this man in front of him.

"I see," nodded Harry. "But now if this is all a lie and Chattock comes gaily driving through Old Twistibus, and gets here—where am I?"

"Damn it to hell," snapped DiValo, "he won't come driving through, I tell you, because—well, simply because of all the circumstances I've cited, and the same being true. All right. What about it? Yes or no—no or yes?" Harry spoke gently.

"DiValo, you've put me on the strangest spot a human being ever was put on. However, you've given me permission to at least elicit from Melody the fact that he went away to look into the possible existence of some marriage record. And if she confirms that, then I'll do this thing *if* and *providing* you give me one reason—one!—why I should take upon myself this grave responsibility. Only in that event will I do it. That you give me—that one reason."

"I'll give you two," said DiValo scornfully. "The first you've had already: that you're to do this thing—perfectly, and in the full manner described—because you've committed the crime of bigamy in a state where they deal out 5 years for that crime—and because the Attorney-General of that state would see that you got it—and would make it stick. And the other reason—"

And now DiValo drew forth from his dressing-gown breast pocket a large, sealed, addressed, and flamboyantly stamped envelope, which he held silently up, its address turned toward the other. Harry the Skeleton leaned forward to view it, and it became evident, by the way his tired eyes suddenly stuck forth from his skull-like head, that he at last knew that DiValo was not playing with words!

For, as DiValo himself knew, there was printed on the face of the big envelope, in large hand-printed lettering, the name of "Daniel DeLong Dee, Attorney-General," and below it the words "care the Courts," together with an address.

"This epistle," explained DiValo amiably, "contains the facts of your peregrinations into matrimony—plus our exact route, for weeks ahead, and is to be mailed up town the very second you don't carry through this thing, in the exact manner outlined—*or* at any moment thereafter during such time when Melody and I are still with the show, that anything shows itself to have 'leaked.' Now is this last a good reason—all in itself?"

"Both the reasons you've just cited," said the Living Skeleton wearily, "are good. In fact," he added, with what sounded like almost a groan, "they're not just good; they're—they're perfect!"

CHAPTER XII

WANTED: ONE WINE-CHEMIST

Willie-Willie Noon, his sunbrowned face shaven clean, thanks to the wooden-handled razor left him by his paw, his coarse, almost gorilla-fur-like brown hair shingled roughly by the same instrument, held up the tiny thimblelike glass of dark red wine which he had accepted—merely as a courtesy—from Miz' Cres'fiel'.

Willie-Willie felt none of the uneasiness today that he customarily felt in her presence, even though he was an ancient of 40, for on this date of his biggest gift to this hopeless love of his life, his black-and-white-striped hickory shirt was impeccably clean from having been washed out, late this very morning, in a brook, even ironed out smoothly atop a piece of shale by a round, hot stone; his sun-faded overalls, ragged at the ends of their short legs, and one leg even shorter than the other, were likewise clean, thanks to the same washing process, if not the ironing one.

Saxone Crestfield—or Miz' Cres'fiel' herself!—in the little parlour of the cottage at 5-Mile Point, was a perfect contrast to Willie-Willie. For the flowered seersucker dress, with flaring skirt, that she wore, was one made in a big city for people who want to play at gardening; and her golden hair was coiffured by herself exactly as done in beauty parlours in the East.

"No, Willie-Willie," she was saying, "I can't figure out for you the kind of wine it is. Much as I truly wish I could help you. It seems, somehow, to barely suggest elderberry—yet I would say also, strangely, that there's a taste in it of a wine that I've encountered only in London—being fermented from a berry that grows only in damp climates like the British Isles."

"'Shaw, Miz' Cres'fiel'," Willie-Willie shook his head positively, "my maw couldn' never ha' gottened nothin' like that. Whatev' she made it out'n, she made it f'm things what grows hyar in this valley."

"Or some strange seedlets—brought in by someone—don't forget," she laughed. "If, as you say, you were gone that whole summer it was made."

She said no more for the moment, but set her completely emptied glass down on the oval gatelegged table, close to the now loosely-corked glass bottle which Willie-Willie had just brought. He now set his untasted thimblelike glass down alongside.

"I feel guilty, Willie-Willie," she protested, "that I can't help you—when you've brought me, for myself alone, one of the only three bottles of this wonderful—this—this truly divine nectar, that you've got—well, two now, isn't it, since you drank up one when you found them?"

"'Shaw, Miz' Cres'fiel'," expostulated Willie-Willie hastily, "I want 'at you should have it. Hain't I got me one more bottle back t' home in my cabin fer to give m' bride—when'ver in tarnation I ketch one? But I shore wisht 'at I could figger what Maw made that 'air wine out'n. I—I could make up some myse'f. And I'd have me so'thin' what people'd mebbe come a long way fur."

"I believe that, Willie-Willie. There's an old aphorism you know, about if a man who makes a better mousetrap than others, people will wear a path—"

"Oh," Willie-Willie interrupted her hastily, "I hain't figga'in' to go in no mousetrap bus'ness, Miz' Cres'fiel'. 'Caount we hain't no mouses p'oblyem in this hyar valley. We got so durned little to eat, y' know—we—we kin scratch so little out'n them dirt spots atween ever'thin'—that ef'n a man he's got mouses or rats eyein' his vittles, he jest posts one o' his young-'uns 'ith a club, to set up all night near whar his vittles is kep'."

He saw her smile broadly, and knew that she did not believe his quite truthful story. "And what," she said, still smiling, "happens if a—a young-'un goes to sleep? And the mouses get into the—the vittles?"

"He gits whopped to a inch of his life," said Willie-Willie.

"But about your nectar here, Willie-Willie. What you need is a wine-chemist."

"A wine—chemis'?" Willie-Willie saw from her nod that he had fairly, or at least fairly accurately, repeated her strange term. "What's 'at?"

"Why—why a wine-chemist is a man who not only tests wine—tests it, I mean, with—with chemicals and—and tools—but who has to taste hundreds of competitor wines, in the course of his work, and thus learns by the very sense of taste to know what's in a wine."

A couple of Miz' Cres'fiel's words—"chemical" and "competitor"—rattled futilely against the back wall of Willie-Willie's comprehension, then bounced away. But he did not need their meaning to drive straight to the point of *that* argument!

"Whar in thund'ation, Miz' Cres'fiel', 'd I ev' git a-holt of a wine-chemis' in these yere parts?"

"Nowhere and never, I'll freely admit, Willie-Willie," she replied quite frankly. "No, Willie-Willie, I only stated what you require. To solve your—your particular enigma. But here!—" She reached down to the cross-piece of the oval gatelegged table, and brought up a pretty sunbonnet in green cloth, trimmed with flowered orange material, "I'll run out now and get you those strawberries for your grandmother—I'm sure there's all of half a hundred left."

Now she drew open the endmost drawer of the table and from it extracted a small flat cardboard box. "Enough, I'm sure," she went on, "to about fill this—which will be ideal for your carrying them that long distance. My goodness," she finished, closing the drawer and turning back to him, "to think of a woman 106 years old even being able to be delighted by an article of food. It's—it's impossible."

"Grammer 'uz alwuz crazy 'bout strawburrys," Willie-Willie endeavoured to explain, without, however, explaining the particular phenomenon at all. "But mo'-so's now'days 'caze hain't no teeth in her haid—not one!"

Miz' Cres'fiel' was putting on her sunbonnet now.

"How long," she asked curiously, "will it take you to get to her place? On—you call it Dead Man's Knob?"

Willie-Willie's face fell. He threw a troubled glance out of the window at his "clock." Which was the slant of the early afternoon sun—the slope and position of a tree shadow. He read the time unerringly, by both.

"That's whar I got to git a wiggle on," he said quite simply. "Fer ef'n I don't git thar befo' darkness makes me lose m' trail, the skeeters'll eat me up t'night. Yep,"—he shook his head firmly—" I gotta make it by dusk—or I'm a dead man."

"Couldn't you—couldn't you camp all night—with a smudge fire?"

"Could, yes'm," he admitted. "An' I a'mit I'd do that befur I'd let m'self be et up. But p'int is 'at t'day—'at is, sundown t'day, or not much later—is the time I gotta be at Crammer's."

"You've got an awful—an awful trek—safari—whatever one would call it!—in front of you. So I'll run out at once and get the berries so you can start."

And off she went out the front door. Now Willie-Willie, alone, walked up and down worriedly. "Hurry, hurry, Miz' Cres'fiel'," he urged, though to himself alone, but perhaps sensing the existence of some kind of mental telepathy. "Fur I shore got to git goin'—or else!"

And here it was that the phone on the wall tinkled. He went over and answered it. More to relieve his own tension.

"Miz' Cres'fiel's house," he intoned. "At 5-Mile P'int." And then added: "Willie-Willie speakin'."

"Willie-Willie—Noon?" came a man's friendly voice. "Why, say— you're the very man I want to speak to. Miss Crestfield could have told me what I want to know—but you can do even better."

"Who be you, mister?"

"Me? Oh, I'm a circus-driver with the MacWhorter Shows. Trailing the show with a truck that—that had to be repaired. Yes, I'm talking from Elum's now—not Cedarville nor Pricetown."

"I know 'at from th' ring. So strong like. Yes, I seed yore show, mister, las' night. For I was t' Pricetown yest'day to see it, an' to visit my brother, who lives thar. I—but 'bout nobody answerin' hyar. Now me, I on'y done got hyar to Miz' Cres'fiel's five minutes ago."

"I see. But here's the point, Mr. Noon. I—"

"Mister—Noon? Willie-Willie, please. Hain't nev' be'n called Mister in m' life."

"Okay, Willie-Willie. Well, I'm just about to start down into the Valley. I'm waiting a longdistance phone call from a city in the north about a business matter—something mighty important to me, and I've got to stick here till I get it!—but then, after I get it, and after settling my phone bill with these good folks, I expect to—to step on it. Mr. Elum here tells me, however, that he and his wife saw you go by early this morning, probably before sun-up, with the circus—that is, riding in one of the seats with one of the drivers, and thinks that you may have been guiding my chief to some—some improvised vehicle bridge that you were figuring to throw across some—well they call it Catamount Creek. Which would save me—so they say!—a full hour's travel. So-o-o—I rang up Miss Crestfield's phone at his suggestion—to see which way the circus may have gone at some fork just beyond her place so as to find out—and lo!—I get *you*—the man who was to throw the bridge across. So-o-o-o—if you were guiding Mr. MacWhorter to this bridge—how'd you like to let me use it this afternoon?"

"But, Mister, they hain't no bridge 'crost Cat'mount Creek. 'Cep'n the little swingin' foot-bridge what's always b'en thar. So I cain't he'p you, see?"

"Well, well, well! Then I shall have to follow Old Twistibus to the letter, I see."

"How long y' figga'in' fo' to git yorese'f t' Fol's'burg?"

"We-ell, I got to be there before show-close tonight—which is around 10:30 or so."

"You should ought to make it afore even show-openin'. Y' got nothin' to worry 'bout."

"No, I suppose not. But saving an hour there where you are—or wherever that bridge was to have been—might have cancelled out some hour I'd lose later. Well, sorry I troubled you—and I'll hang up now so's to be ready to get my call when it comes through. Please accept, then, just the same, the thanks of this humble wine-chemist, and—"

"Wh'—uh—whut's 'at y' said, mister?"

"Humble? Or—or wine-chemist? Why—"

"Wine—chemis'—'d you say you wuz? Or am I twisted like in m' haid?"

"Why, yes, I mean, wine-chemist *is* what I said—not that you're twisted anywhere. Wine-chemist, yes. That's my profess—ah—business. I'm just driving for the MacWhorter Shows for my health. I—"

"Glor—eee—hallyloojy, mister! Now I'm goin' t' b'lieve in mir'cles fer all th' rest o' my life. On'y fi' minutes ago, Miz' Cres'fiel'—she's the lady book nov'list whut lives here—"

"Yes, I know. I'd like to have been able to meet her—but it won't be necessary now. Go ahead?"

"Well, on'y fi' minut's ago, Miz' Cres'fiel' she say to me, 'Willie-Willie, hain't nobody in the whol' world but a wine-chemis' kin solve yore problem fer you.'"

"And then one calls up, eh? Well, life is like that, my good friend. It happens all the time—but what is your problem?"

"W'y," poured forth Willie-Willie, "my maw—she's daid, le' me say— she made some wine out'n some berries she growed—or else found in the woods—or else what maybe even got brung in to her. But she made on'y 3 bottles. An' I found 'em on'y las' week, 'ith some p'esarves she put up, in a hidin'-place in the cellar. Well, I drinked one—gawdy, it was good! I drinked that whole bottle afore I re'lized I didn' know what 'twas made f'm."

"Well, what berries grow around your place?"

"Don't know whut growed thar las' summer. Drought kilt ev'thing that fall when I got back. How'ver, Maw she could fin' berries in the woods whut nobody else knowed."

"Yes, I see. Well, you can make wine from a thousand things—even if they don't contain much sugar. I—well did the single bottle you drank kick you? Into, I mean—ah—kingdom come? In short, was your drink strong?"

"Seems like, mister, it made me awful happy like. Full o' plans."

"Oh, yes. High etheric content—but low alcoholic content. Any bitter-ness?"

"Yes, they was. But ef you ast me, 'twas a pleasant kin' o' bitt'ness. Whut give it zip—make you want mo' of it—ef you know what I mean?"

"Yes, I do. Well, bitterness can mean one of two—but you have more of the wine, you say? Two bottles altogether?"

"Wa-all, on'y one, I reckon. I burrit that 'un in m' cabin—what lays sev'al miles on from hyar. T'other, I give to Miz' Cres'fiel'. Fer a present. Fack is I jest give it to her ten minut's or so ago. She says it tastes to her a little bit like eld'berry, but on t'other hand, she says it co'tains a flavey like so'thin' in a wine she drank in London once."

"In London, eh? However, my friend, I'm afraid there are no more undiscovered or unidentified wines today. It's true that I could tell you an amazing lot about your wine. Even, in fact, whether you should follow it up. Understand, I haven't my kit of chemistry tools with me. And you want a professional opinion, don't you?"

"Goshy, mister, d'—d' y' think you could stop by here on yore way, an' sip a glass o' this wine what's all here ready—an's on'y jest b'en opened?"

"Yes, I could. The whole thing wouldn't take me but 5 minutes or so, all in all."

"Gosh, mister, would—would you do that? You've got plenty, plenty time fer to make Fol'sburg—this side o' show-close."

"Yes, I suppose I have. I—in fact, I'll do it. Will you be there waiting for me? I have to wait here at least till I catch a call-back from the north."

"Mister, they hain't no use o' me bein' hyar—w'en you kin tell Miz' Cres'fiel' ev'thing they is to be tolt. Me, I gotta haid like hell fer Dead Man's Knob. Whar my grammer lives. It's a long story, but ef I don't make it afo' dusk I'm—I'm a nigh-dead man from skeeters big as—as el'phants. Minute Miz' Cres'fiel' comes back 'ith the berries, I'm gonna step on it."

"You too, eh? Well, tell the lady the set-up then, and I'll give her, for you, a real off-the-record report as to age, palatability, kick, and everything a wine can have. Including, my friend, a fair hypothesis as to three possible main berries, grapes, or whatnot, that may be in it."

"Thanks a mill'on, mister! An' I say it now, 'caze I won't be seein' you."

"Okay. Explain the set-up, then, when she comes. And tell her I may be by in 15 minutes—*if* all goes well. It all depends on how soon my call—"

But here came an interruption on the wire. "Mist' Man at Blum's? This—this is Ced'ville. It's 'bout yore call f'm Wine City. Now a sho't stretch o' line what c'nnects some lines in the nawth 'ith these lines down hyar goin' east-west, is full up 'ith a big local polit'cal conf'rence goin' ovah it. An's due to be in use fer all o' two hours yit. But onder th' line reg'lations, they hatter give up the sarcu't five minut's evv'y hour, ef'n an'body's tryin' to git th'ough, an' so they'll be gittin' off in 'zackly 45 minutes' time. An' yore Mist' Kirkaldy he's be'n 'ssigned the 5-minute gap. So-o-o, ef you'll be standin' by—I'll repo't all's in read'ness. Will you be?"

"Whew! 45 minutes yet, eh? Sure, I'll be right here. I'll just have to make it up afterward. But don't forget, that's all."

"'Caount on it comin' th'ough raght on th' dot, in that there 5-minute gap," the girl said confidently, and was off the circuit. Chattock was speaking again.

"Well, Willie-Willie, you heard?—so it's darned well you aren't trying to wait for *me!* Good luck to you, on your trip to your granny's."

Chattock hung up, and Willie-Willie turned from the phone, rubbing his brown gnarled hands in satisfaction, in getting a report on his precious wine. Scarcely two seconds later, Miz' Cres'fiel' herself bustled in, the small striped cardboard box in her hands, and stapled tight at its fastening.

"Here they are, Willie-Willie," she cried. "At least 50 of them. Luscious, too. You'll have to take my word for it, for after washing them I laid them out in the box here, and the berries fit and fill it. All in readiness they are now to carry. Your grandmother should be delighted—if she really likes strawberries. I hope so, anyway."

She had flung her sunbonnet on a nearby chair as she talked. He swept quickly over to where his jagged rimmed hat lay on the floor, came over to her, and took the box of berries eagerly.

"Thanks a mill'on, Miz' Cres'fiel'. Grammer'll 'caount me her fav-rite gran'son now. An'—but I'm gonna fly, an' how! And so whut I got to say, I got to say fas'! Miz' Cres'fiel', I 'uz jes' talkin' on yore phone to a sarcus-driver who's a-fetchin' th'ough a sarcus truck f'm Pricetown—he's at Elum's now—and, by crickey, he's—he's a wine-chemis'!"

"A—wine-chemist?" she exclaimed. "Why-heaven must have dropped him right in your—how do you know?"

"Oh, him an' me we had a long gab on th' wire. Though I nev' did git his name. He's b'en drivin' on'y fer his health. And he is a wine-chemis'. An', Miz' Cres'fiel', he's a-goin' to stop off hyar. An' Willie-Willie Noon's face grew apologetic. "You—you won't 'ject, will ya, to s'pply him one glass of yore bottle fer his pu'pose? He—he needs a whole glass."

"Heavens no, Willie-Willie! There's more there than I could drink in a month of Sundays or—go ahead?"

"Well, he say he kin tell a heap o' things 'bout it whut he kin tell you to tell me. He—he say he kin someday brag 'at he oncet met the lady writer of a book novel famous all over the world."

"That's crossing a bridge far ahead of time, Willie-Willie. And one that, alas, may never come to be. Why, my publisher-to-be may say there are no such people—such as you folks here!"

"How," he asked gravely and pointedly, "kin he say that when they is? Don't make no sense to me, fer—but whew!—I'm a-goin'. An'—an' I'll be back hryar day aft' t'morrow. An' ef you don't mind tellin' me then all whut this feller tells you 'bout my wine—"

"No, no, not at all. Run on! I'll convey it all faithfully. I hope he isn't conveying some sick tigress or something—I'd be frightened stiff if I thought one was even standing in its wagon cage, out in front of my—what is the reason," she broke off puzzledly, "or didn't he say?—why he's trailing his show so far behind? Yet has to so positively join it—before show-close?"

Willie-Willie stood, hand on door-jamb, thinking.

"Miz' Cres'fiel'," he said with sudden impulsiveness, "don't you skeer yo'rese'f one little bit 'bout no tigress nor nothin' settin' out in front yore place durin' that wine-tastin'. No, he didn't tell me the w'y o' all this—but it jest happens I know, see? 'Caze o' bein' at Hick'ry's yist'day an' 'twell 'arly this mo'nin', an' Hick'ry—Hick'ry bein' the town banker there t' Pricetown. This hyar truck he's a-fetchin' through hain't a reg'lar sarcus wagon, see? Hit's a ord'n'y white trock 'ith on'y the sarcus name lettered on it. 'Caze it's a so-called office truck, see? It's got a safe fixed in it som'way in th' back— whar it cain't be seed ner nothin'—on'y it's one o' these hyar de—posit safes whut kin be opened on'y by corr—corr—corr—"

"Correspondent banks, you mean?" she helped out.

"'At's right," he nodded. "In th' safe o' this 'tic'ler system, they's both a combyanation an' a key i'volved. An' this hyar safe, Miz' Cres'fiel', it's now got in it three thousan' dollars what cain't be emptied out 'twell Fol'sburg. Whar, it seems, they's 'nother corr'spondy bank, see? Hick'ry he b'en takin' good care of the truck in his garagy 'twell the driver could git thar. Fer this driver, Miz' Cres'fiel'—yes, the wine-chemis' feller!—he wa'n't one of the sarcus men left ahind ner nothin', fer Mist' MacWhorter he 'uz bad up ag'in it fer drivers—no, this feller was somewhar in the nawth, an' he 'uz to fly down to Nosebag Fiel' east an' south o' Pricetown, lope on t' Pricetown by bus, an' pick up this truck this mo'nin' at 11. New wheel an' all a'ready on it, see, fer a suttin old clown whut was lef ahind to 'dentify this feller—well, this here ol' clown 'uz to git the wheel w'en it come down f'm Wheel City on the mornin' train at 10 o'clock, an' put it on the truck all in read'ness fer the feller's pickin' it up at 11. Aft' which, this here old clown 'uz to go into the hospital thar for some kind o' opyration. He—but that," finished Willie-Willie triumphantly, "is th' inside o' this feller's trailin' the show so late. And havin' to git thar afore show-close. An' so you won't have to worry yore pretty haid 'bout fierce animiles standin' in front of yore place in cages nor nothin'. On'y—what I've tolt you is strickly atween you an' me, Miz' Cres'fiel'. You—well, I'm off," he broke off.

And off he was. Out the door, off the porch, and weaving around the side of the house toward a thicket in the rear where he could immediately and unerringly pick the foot-trail that would start to take him countless miles straight south.

He would have been a surprised Willie-Willie, however, had he, as he moved with great loping strides across the open space toward the thicket, seen Miz' Cres'fiel's actions after he had left. For after first standing help-lessly riveted where he had left her—riveted apparently by all this informa-tion which she apparently could not believe—she turned and locked the door through which he had come and gone. Now she crossed the parlour quickly, and opened a door which gave into an ascetically-furnished dining-room, plainly not used by her, for its two windows were down, and locked tightly. She closed this door, and turned immediately to the wall beside it where a stout ladder, nailed firmly thereto, supplied the stairway to the attic which obviously had never been built in this house.

Up the ladder she went with sureness and firmness; the sureness and firmness, no less, of much practice. Clear to the trapdoor at its top she ascended. Where, however, instead of shoving it open with the palm of one hand, she knocked.

Knocked once. Twice! Three times! Then a space, and a fourth knock.

To the rattling sound of several bolts and whatnot, it was suddenly opened. Gingerly, however—about a foot—no more. But at least enough for her to step up another rung of the ladder and raise her blue eyes far enough over floor-level to take in what might be thus revealed to her gaze, which proved to be just a well-swept attic floor, with a canvas cot over to one side, a partly-filled quart bottle of whisky by its side, and some magazines loosely atop it as evidenced by the end of one, the corner of another, protruding over the canvas edge.

The reason the trapdoor remained open, however, and only partly so, was because there was a hand firmly on one edge of it; and visible upward through the opening was a man of about 44, with a very slight growth of beard, dressed in a belted soft white silk shirt, and wearing woolly noiseless slippers.

"It's okay, Steve," she said gaily. "Oh yes, the hick's gone. Steve, let me in quick—else get the knock-out drops from the black bag, and shove them down to me here. Yes, that's what I said—the knockout drops. For our long period of hiding out here, after your Tulsa bank job, is over—we've a perfect 'out' from this place, in spite of all those pics of you all over the southwest here, and no mazuma to boot—we've—listen, Stevie, there's a piece of change on its way here in a truck, a fortune of 3 grand. 3 grand, Stevie! 3 grand—say, swing that thing back and let your baby in! It's an absolute 'natural.' The biggest 'natural' that ever flew into the laps of two jug mobsters on the lam."

She seated herself on an empty soap-box placed next the canvas cot, her shapely legs crossed without reserve, the man himself, still hard and cold blue of eye, on his back, his hands underneath his head, his knees drawn up. He listened as she explained.

"He's all set to stop off and drink one full glass of wine that he knows already will have a slight bitter taste—can have *any* taste, so far as that goes, since its sources are absolutely unknown—set, also, incidentally, to meet one lady novelist whom he thinks he may like!—and hasn't the remotest idea that the secret of that white truck has been blabbed into the possession of two jug mobsters who haven't a penny on earth, but have one trustworthy sidekick in Little Rock, Arkansaw, who can pop that gopher in the secrecy of his stone garage like nobody's business."

"Don't ramble now, Blueing-Eyes," the man cut in. "For time's a-passing! It all is a natural, all right, all right: not only a natural, however, but one of those one-in-a-million naturals. For with him snoring away, we *can* get out of this awful graveyard after dark falls tonight—you inside the truck, and me outside driving—and if anybody whatsoever spots the truck rolling swiftly back eastward, they'll just figure that it encountered something wrong in Old Twistibus, like a bridge down or something, and is having to head back to—"

"—only," she helped out, "we turn off—ahead of Pricetown!"

"Yes!" he said fervently. "Rather. But turning off by the more or less unused Cactus Pike stretch, we'll have only 25 miles to negotiate. After which, we'll be on the hard sweet road that'll—"

"—the hard sweet road on which," she declared quite firmly, "you will be inside the truck—and little old me, in pants and shirt, on the seat. Oh, yes. For gal truck-drivers are nothing in this part of the country—but hot bank-heisters, drawing into the outskirts of a big burg—"

"Okay, okay," he cut in. "That suits me. The point I'm musing about particularly is that that hard sweet road will put us into Little Rock by dawn. Where—"

"Before dawn, easy, Stevie!" she corrected. "Before dawn, easy! You're going by an over-all mental picture of this great Southwest region here—but I've been measuring the roads out from here, in the atlas I found here, with a ruler, for a week. We'll be in Little Rock long before dawn. I should be ringing up Ehoff Matray, from some outlying all-night drugstore, in that cushy hotel where he kips out, a full hour before dawn cracks in the east—ringing him up to get the hell out to Mud Flats, and open up that stone garage he keeps there with nothing in it."

"Okay, Blueing-Eyes, since you've measured everything out with a ruler. I wonder," he broke off, "what that little son-of-a-bitch of an Ehoff will demand for popping that gopher?"

"Since he won't have any heat over his head while he does the job—being able, in short, to take his fool time with his one wing—he'll think he's paid swell if he catches half a grand out of it. Yes, a half a grand—"

"—leaving two and a half for us, eh, Sweetkins?" nodded the man, suddenly enthused, plainly, by the practical possibilities in this thing. "Two and a half grand immediately available, and completely unidentifiable mazuma, which—babe, the more I think on this, the more I'm convinced I'm having a dream. It's—it's not possible."

"It's not only possible," she pointed out, businesslike, "but in the taking of this guy's 3 grand—rather, his boss's to be exact—we catch the means of getting ourselves out of this damned trap we've gotten ourselves into. His truck, I mean."

She said no more, but stepped over back of the end of the cot, and from one of two bags standing there drew one forth where some of the daylight from the end attic window could illumine it, snapped it open and from it, mostly full of feminine things, extracted a small metal-capped bottle of whitish-looking liquid. This she tucked down into a pocket of her seersucker dress. During all of this, he had sprung up, and going over to the trapdoor, now held it open for her. She returned to it now, and stepped gingerly down atop the ladder, helped by his one free hand. Now she was descending, smiling up at him as he, the ever-cautious one, closed the trap and shot the bolts.

CHAPTER XIII

THREE WHO WAITED

The three men who, with poised and carefully-directed machine-gun in the hands of one, sat, lay, or squatted behind the gargantuan, half-sunken, weather-beaten boulder alongside Old Twistibus, Idiot's Valley, were not hillbillies by any manner of means. Indeed, they would have been decreed to be, by an astute F.B.I. man from a big city, hard men of the country post office safe-cracking type. Killers who, in their day, had "bumped" more than one "town hack." One, who sat back firmly against the boulder, was pockmarked, swarthy, and plainly Mexican. He was about 40, and wore wrinkled, crumpled, dirty brown trousers, belted, by a tattered, frayed, black leather belt, to a silk shirt which once had been glaringly crimson but today was dirt-encrusted, sweat-stained, red-black instead of crimson.

Had this man's gaze, toward a thicket thick with high-grown weeds between its trees, been a seeing gaze instead of a completely abstracted non-seeing one, it would have taken in a single feature that could have been viewed only from the precise position where he himself sat. That feature was a single gap, or slot, in a cunning camouflage curtain of weeds and green grass built across the thicket, but in which gap could be seen just the rearmost corner of a Ford car with bamboo fishpoles sticking out and bespeaking "fishermen"! The one of the three men who reclined lazily at full length behind the boulder, but slightly off from it and the Mexican, was an obvious Jap, with extraordinarily oblique black eyes, but framed by thick lenses that would have been more logical on a Prussian face. There was a single square black leather case near his feet which he seemed to guard ever so carefully, at least as to its being removed, overturned, or even put into position to be jostled by someone, for every now and then he tried out its position gently with the toe first of one foot, then the other, in such a way that it was plain he could not even see that far with his myopic eyes.

The third man, who squatted on his heels at the further edge of the huge blob of mineral matter—squatted behind the machine-gun, in fact—was stocky of shoulders, about 40 years of age, and possessed of cold, blue, unmistakable "killer's" eyes. He wore a dirty green-flannel shirt, open at his sunbrowned neck, and suspendered by mis-matched braces on to equally dirty khaki trousers, and by the way he held on to, and guided the machine-gun, he demonstrated the impropriety of anyone's saying the weapon was "in his hands." For only one hand did he have, and that one on the firing and directing mechanism of the gun: the other "hand" was a handless stump which, however, he kept firmly across the gun-breech as though to help in directing and manipulating the weapon.

Now and again, could one have watched him minutely, and over a pro-tracted period, one would have seen him adjust the weapon meticulously upon its pivot, a quarter inch this way—a quarter that way—as though to assure himself ever of its complete maneuverability; but the fixed gaze of his cold blue eyes, through the chink in the verdure concealing him and his gun, could be seen to be ever on the width of grey ribbon that was the road. Proving completely that he was not waiting for a crow to alight in a tree, nor a blackbird to pose himself upon a hillock.

Now the Mexican, drawing irritably on his unlighted cigarette as though it were lighted, asked peevishly:

"I steel don' see, Chief, w'y you got blow theez faller to hell an' go, th' meenut he show. W'y for you no at leas' try shout 'Halt,' an' see what hap-pen?"

"Because, you idiot," the man back of the gun said angrily, turning his eyes away momentarily from the slit through which he peered, and to the speaker, "he's gatted up, I tell you, and ready to let fly himself with a tommy-gun or an automatic jerked out pronto from under his behind—the second he catches a command like *that*. You don't believe that mullarky that Spearfish—as he now confesses—plucked out of the carbon copy of that let-ter he picked up in the telegraph office, do you?—I mean, about this 3 grand being taken through Old Twistibus here all casual-like and on the q.t.? Why, that simple, easy set-up was painted in that letter by the circus-owner, for the bozo in the north, so's the latter wouldn't get his wind up. And ju-u-ust maybe decide not to come on. No, that clown that was left behind gave the guy from the north his real instructions all right, all right—*and* his necessary artillery! Anee-body who shouts 'halt' this day of June the 13th, along this p't'c'ler stretch of road, to the baby on the white truck—transporting not peanuts but three grand—is going to be sprayed with slugs before he can say Jack Robinson."

"But, Slicer," put in the Jap troubledly, but in perfect English, "the truck may go so badly out of control, with a dead man at the wheel, that—"

"Yeah?—and turn over, perhaps—and so what? 'Twon't run *you* boys down, behind this 20-ton pebble. Nor me either—for I'll be sitting on your laps when she begins to go haywire! So what worries you, Slant-Eyes?

That you may have to blow a hole in her side in case she's lying atop some door—and Mex can't kick it in with the sledge?"

"I am not worried," said the thick-spectacled Jap proudly—with the supreme pride of a super-technician in his own line—"about *any* soup job where I can work close, and know exactly what I'm supposed to do. Just so long as one of you can lead me to the spot where I'm to do my stuff."

"Oh, we will!" said the stocky-shouldered man. "We will. As a matter of fact, your short vision will be an asset for you. For in that way you won't see a certain pair of dead glims reproachfully watching what you do. Oh, not the driver, no. No, a dead man who'll have been inside that truck all the time, with a tommy-gun of his own." He laughed curtly, a sort of contemptuous laugh. "I didn't want to tell you boys before that we're almost certainly up against a carefully and downright guarded truck today. But that clown that's supposed to have stayed on there in Pricetown to turn the truck over to the guy from the north and then go on to a hospital—hell fire, he isn't going to any hospital to get cut up. He's a bodyguard, scheduled to travel ri-i-ight along inside the truck, with a tommy-gun of his own ready to lay to a hole drilled in either side. That whole truck is going to be sprayed like rain with steel-jacketed slugs before either one knows what happens."

"Boy," said the Mexican, almost admiringly, "whan Oncle Sam he put you in the Armee to keel Germans, he—"

"'At's right, Mex," said the stocky-shouldered man sardonically. "I killed so many dozen—hundreds—thousands of 'em in that war, that it's as natural today for me to lay slugs in carcasses as it is to toss BB shots into dough."

He turned his gaze to the muzzle of his machine-gun. All was silence. Silence broken only by the caw of a distant, seemingly far-distant, crow: the flap of a buzzard's wing, off to the north, and not even sailing over the three men.

The Mexican, taking his cigarette from his mouth, sighed.

"I know you theenk me a sent'mental fool," he said apologetically. "But I no can forgat that driver. I no theenk there be any clown eenside—but driver I dam' well know be on seat. An' I kind of sorree for that faller. Wan meenut he rolleeng along road—pas' bee-oot-iful boulder, like—he will be wheestleeng, mabbe, like hell—sweet mooseec!—theenking of his girl eef he got one—an'—"

"—and two seconds later," said the stocky-shouldered, khaki-trousered man caustically, "he's knocking at the Pearly Gates. What the hell—and this goes for the both of you. When you consider how all three of us have got to check out some day—by rope—chair—or gas chamber—we're being mi-i-ighty nice and easy for this bully-boy on the truck seat. Werry gen'rous, if you ask *me*. We—"

The speaker stopped short. Plucked from a pocket, with his good hand, a silver watch. Glanced at it, then popped it back. Put his good hand immediately back on the gun-breech, his eyes on the road.

"All right now," he said curtly, suddenly businesslike. "Pipe down—both of you. No more gassing! For according to the way *I* figure things, if he left Pricetown at 11 A.M. as he was set to do, he'd have got to Elum's about 12 noon or a little after. And assuming he took a noon hour there—put the nosebag on, say, and chewed the rag with the Elums—he'd have started on down into the Valley about 1:30 at most. And if he did this, then, according to my reckoning, he'll be here now in 10—20—perhaps 30 minutes at most. So quiet now, all of you. And get ready—to see some fireworks!"

CHAPTER XIV

THE MAN WITH THE PAPER NOSE

Ludicrous, to say the least, was the figure who sat in Melody Ashbrooke's trailer, at 6:30 of the evening that the show was to play Foleysburg. For the figure, in addition to being clad in monstrously loose flapping garments made of material carrying alternate black and white circles as big as saucers, the coat of which was comically far too short, as were the trousers also, had a face make-up such as probably had never before been seen on land nor sea!

For he wore a long paper nose with a brilliant crimson tip, and under it, glued to his upper lip by some adhesive, a mammoth and brushlike red walrus moustache. So artfully blended had been the base of the paper nose to the face wearing it, by skin-coloured paint or putty, that it looked exactly like a real proboscis. One eye of the red walrus-moustached figure had been blackened in a great patch, covering all of the socket, so that he resembled, in some respects, a sad Skye terrier. On the figure's head was a skintight bald-headed man's wig with, however, an unkempt fringe of fiery red hair around the edge where it joined his own scalp, and atop the shiny dome, though well to one side as though ready to topple off any minute, was a tiny brown derby hat not much bigger than a coffee cup.

Melody herself sat back in her chair. She was clad just now in a little green velvet dress—her walk-about-grounds dress, she always called it!—with hem falling decorously just below her shapely knees, its elbow-length sleeves puffed in shape, and with a modest jewelled buckle at the waist.

"Jules!" she cried. "It—it's side-splitting! However did you devise it—and where did you get the elements?"

"Had 'em," Jules DiValo said gravely. "Had 'em—amongst my stuff. And wanted you to see how I'm going to do the act in the night clubs. And—as at least I thought when I put it on—tonight on the platform, for one wouldn't ordinarily bother to change at this late moment. The old-fashioned stuff of doing magic in tails and all, is over. MacWhorter is hopelessly— God, yes, hopelessly!—old-fashioned. Tails have been overdone, not just by card-rifflers, but by ventriloquists, club-tossers, M.C.s—everything. Till they—they stink—if you'll pardon my Anglo-Saxon, honey?—they stink, for giving the audience a kick. Now the people in a night club are bored. They wouldn't be there, paying minimum and cover-charges and all, if they weren't so bored that they—well, when you stand in the wings of the little stage of a night club, waiting to come on, you're waiting to come on to an audience that already is fighting you, before you've even stepped on, with its own boredom; with its complete expectation that one more canary—in long velvet dress and sleeves, and a single necklace!—is ready to slither on, or another maestro in tails to do whatever it is he's going to do. But, honey, if you—that is, an artist like me!—can lope out on to that stage in such an unexpected guise that—well, that he throws 'em all at one time into one giant roar of laughter, that comes from the sheer unexpectedness of the get-up as much as the get-up itself, then the act is yours from then on. You've won—hands down!" The girl shook her head.

"It's really side-splitting, Jules. It should make them laugh quite outside of any unexpectedness in it. It—well when you came in, I was plenty down in the dumps, I admit. And if you made *me* laugh, it—it must be good!"

"Don't be down in the dumps," he said soothingly. "Think of the future—instead of the past—or the much abused what-might-have-been. The future—our future—but that, honey, is what I really came over about just now. Our future."

"What do you mean, Jules? I thought that was all arranged now."

"Honey," he said, "*I* just learned good news. Rather, a whole heap of good news, all more or less accidental. Oh, no, I don't mean the simple matter about the show opening a bit later than customary tonight because of that fool stuff up town—no, I mean that I just learned that there's a 'mail-totin' auto-mobile' that goes out every evening from the Foleysburg P.O. to Fenster Crossing—yes, where we were going to hoof it to tonight. His car is an old Lincoln, with plenty of capacity, and so he carries passengers to Fenster Crossing—at $1 each. And, last but not least—and here is where I must step on things!—he goes out in 45 minutes from now. And—but here's what I'm driving at. Why not toss our stuff, in the next 15 minutes, into our two respective suitcases, then amble quietly over, by way of the back limits of the lot here, to the P.O. which is no more than the length of two city blocks from where we sit right now and go out northward with him. On the cushions, in short, instead of by shanks' mare—uh—by leg-work."

"But, Jules," the girl expostulated, "what good would it do? We'd only have to be dropped off at some clergyman's, on the way, there to have to sit and wait, in his parlour, or on his front porch, until I am technically 21 by the papers which I have. For only then, after all, am I 100 per cent free of residence requirements in this state."

"No," he put in hurriedly. "For one thing, that crossing-agent and flagman at Fenster Crossing is no other than—well, he's the clergyman for that region around there. And does the other only as a sideline. No, we'll dive straight through to his place."

"But still, what good would it do?" she expostulated. "I'd still have to sit on his porch, or a station bench, waiting till I was 21. Therefore, I might just as well stay back here, and do my stint tonight for Mr. MacWhorter. Remember, I faithfully told Bill, in that letter I sent him to Chicago, that I would not leave this show till show-close—of *this day.*"

"But what on heaven and earth," he cried, "has Bill got to do with it—now? He was disposed of completely, it seems to me."

"Yes, I know," she admitted. "I know. He told Harry he hadn't been successful—had failed, in short—in that mission whose outcome I admit I had very little hope for myself. *If* any at all. Since—but, Jules—there's always the possibility that Bill told Harry all that for some strange reason—well, Bill has a great sense of the dramatic in his soul, you know. He—well, the point is that if he told Harry that—including that he wasn't coming back to the show— he—he may have done so just to—to heighten some dramatic effect he might make by walking into the show by show-close. Oh well, there's the matter of *my* word of honour—he *may* have depended fully on it—he may come walking in—"

"With *what?*" the man said almost angrily. "With what? The full explanation of why he failed? Or a—a plea to you that he'll never eye you scornfully and contemptuously over the breakfast table, some morning years hence, as illegitimate? With what, honey, will he come walking in?"

"Well, if—if he does come in this way—dramatically, in short, he—it—it will be—would be with the proof that my mama and papa were married."

Jules DiValo threw up his hands.

"I—give up!" he said. "I—give up. Here, Harry gives us the lowdown that he got from Bill, the lowdown that Bill has failed—and now you postulate that Bill may just be—be being dramatic—be laying for a dramatic scene—Bluebeard's wife's brother galloping down the road to save her."

She stopped him. "Call it then just a matter of my word of honour—no matter what he is. Namely, that I told Bill I would stay here till show-close."

"If you could have heard," he said grimly, shaking his red-fringed head gravely side to side, "Harry's description, to me personally only, of the disgusted, drawn, frustrated look on Bill's face, you would know for sure that he failed completely."

"All I can say," she expostulated, "is that if Bill *doesn't* come in by show-close, then the last possibility is out: namely, that he told all this to Harry—acted it out, drawn face and all—for dramatic purposes, in order to—to later thrill and surprise me. What difference does it make, Jules, whether you and I arrive in Northern Kansas on a caboose before dawn to-morrow—or later? Once there, this life is all over and past—a new life has begun with you—"

"I know," he was the one now to expostulate. "But I see no reason why we should drag this thing—this waiting for Bluebeard's wife's brother, yes!—out further, when the only possibility—namely, that Bill is lurking outside the show, anywhere from 10 miles to 100, just to—to—to deliver a gre-eat, gra-a-and dramatic surprise."

"I know," she smiled. "It's awfully tenuous, isn't it? But remember, Jules, you too agreed farther back there to wait this day, and the hour of show-close today, to give me the chance of his proving Mama's and Papa's marriage. And since—since I was willing, in the absence of same, to embark on a new life with you—and give you the chance to teach me to love—let us," she broke off, "carry through as we arranged, Jules. For I will know then I played fair, to the last detail. Yes, let us carry through as arranged."

"Show-close it is then," the man said. "But he won't be in. You will find his story to Harry was right, all right. And assuming that he came in and had come through Old Twistibus—how would you even have known that the proof he brought—say, a copy of a page from some marriage-register book—was bona fide?"

"Oh, that," she said confidently, "would be easy to establish. For you see, Papa knew the facts and solution of some famous old murder called the Ragpicker Joe Murder. And set them down on the back of that page. In a code that he had invented—if, again, his story to a certain old dying actor when I was about ten years of age were true. And since I mailed Bill the set of rotating alphabetical dials which Papa invented for coding—well, don't you see, Bill would have the solution of that famous old murder? Which would prove that the register-page was there."

"*I* don't even know," said the man, "what the facts of the said murder were. How did your fa—papa get them in the first place?"

"Well, he knew a Goldie—"

"Blonde woman or blondined woman? Which? But go on?"

"—knew this Goldie well. I even have—did have, before I sent it to Bill—a letter of Father's written to this woman—but never finished, see? Only commenced, by 'Dear Goldie,' suggesting thereby that there was at least no love-relationship between them, nor—well, in it Father starts out by mentioning having that day come on a little true-crime-story magazine pur-porting to partly 'explain' the 'findings' of some police investigator named Frank DuShane. Father went on to say, in this letter, that he was led to write to this woman not only by the finding of the little true-crime-story maga-zine, but by the fact that he'd found in some trade-journal dealing with their profession that she was 'alive and kicking,' and that he'd fallen to wondering how she was 'these many years, considerable years later'—that's the way he put it. And then—"

"Yes? Go ahead, honey?"

"Well, then he tells her that the 'facts of that occurrence,' so 'fully confided to him by her,' had never been divulged by him to any living person, and never would be, as long as any of the parties in it are alive. And then Father adds the most sinister thing of all. For he says—and I'm quoting his exact words, Jules—he says 'As for the mere fact that the wielder of the dagger goes about in the world today, free and unrestrained and all that—well, this case is an intricate case, to say the least. And to my mind you are the only one to be considered.' And—well, the letter breaks off not long after that—was never finished. For Papa—Papa died!"

"Well, I'd say," declared the man firmly, "that you didn't even need Bill Chattock—rather, the back of a register-page which we've agreed doesn't exist—to get a lead on this murder which the unfinished letter does at least prove your father knew about. I mean, the woman Goldie. No, I don't even know the circumstances of said murder—yet it seems to me, in my ignorance, that I am able to give you a suggestion by which to catch your lead. And this is it: since Mr. Mac knew your papa also years ago—else you would never have wound up with this show, as you've explained!—since Mr. MacW knew him, as did doubtless hundreds of other people, why don't you just query Mr. MacW, before you pull out, as to who your father's woman friend Goldie might have been? And with what he can probably tell you on that, we might some day—you and I—call on her. And find out the name of the murderer, and—" He made a philosophic gesture. "Or you could decide to keep out of the responsibility of sending someone to the electric chair at this late date."

"Oh," the girl said, "all that I did. I mean," she explained, "ask Mr. MacWhorter out and out if Father had ever mentioned to him, in the days that they knew each other, having a woman friend named Goldie. But he pointed out to me that the period in which he and Father were in more or less close touch with each other was not only years before I was born or—or even thought of—but before he had even started out trying to run this circus on what he called 'a shoestring.' Pointed out even further—and these were his exact words to me, Jules—that any woman friend Father might ever have had could be one of thousands of such he'd have made along the road of life after he, Mr. MacWhorter, and Father were last in touch. Moreover," she emphasized, "when he saw I was sort of frustrated by not getting a lead to this Goldie, he pointed out also the very thing that you did: namely, that the name Goldie has been applied to countless blonde and blondined women in show-business for decades. Oh, I didn't go into details of why I wanted it, since he could throw no light on who this woman Goldie might have been—moreover, he was immersed in his nightly Bible chapter—he thought I was troubled about the possibility of this Goldie being some mistress or something of Father's while Father was with Mother; and he went all out to convince me that Father would never, never have done that. And I let it go at that."

"Well, then," confessed the man, "I'm not so smart as I thought I was. To have imagined you wouldn't at least have tried to get a lead to one former woman friend of your father, via another friend. However, you don't have to sit around waiting for Bill to bring in a—phony solution. Who was killed? Ragpicker Joe, I take it?"

"Yes," she returned quickly. "He was a black-as-coal Negro, unwashed and unbathed. Love, even of the blackest kind, appears to have been completely eliminated by this man DuShane as a motive. Moreover, the very circumstance of the weapon used eliminated anybody Ragpicker Joe consorted with. He was stabbed in the back with a jewelled dagger—a beautiful thing—worth all of $25,000, and never identified. Was found with the dagger driven into his back."

"Well," he conceded, "that does rule the crime out as a revenge-crime in sex, love, or amongst his own people. For his own social circle—assuming even a ragpicker has such!—his own people—just don't possess such trinkets. Where—and when—was he killed?"

"That important thing was more or less obliterated by those who killed him," the girl outlined. "For they took him across the city, in some unknown direction, in a big car—a certain Rolls-Royce-like car seen slithering out of a dark alley alongside, and forming the rear of, a certain small down-at-heel hotel then on the fringe of Chicago's business district, by the night-clerk thereof standing in the doorway of it around 10 P.M., was undoubtedly *the* car—for the district was more or less dilapidated, and not one in which Rolls-Royces customarily visited! They succeeded, by operating from the dark alley, in depositing him in this hotel, in a room they evidently plainly knew was a room delegated just to contain mops, and brooms, and pails."

"Yes, I see," he nodded. "Hm? Well, it looks carefully thought out, all right. And based on advance adroit reasoning. Well, I can only say, my sweet, that I have not seen the weird hotel which made itself the stage for the last act of a murder job, but I claim that you will live to see the case of Ragpicker Joe illuminated and made completely straight. Wait—and see!"

"Wait I shall have to, I fear," said the girl sadly. "Though my desires to know the full inside of it lies only in the matter that I might thus be able to talk to the woman Goldie who must have been involved, if she knew the facts, and who knew Father so intimately. And who might be able to tell me little hidden episodes about him, and my only other chance—namely, that I shall get the inside facts of the case from Bill—Bill, who would have found the marriage-register page and—and decoded the stuff he found on the back!—Bill, dramatically reversing what he told Harry, by coming riding in—striding in—to the show."

And the man shook his skin-tight wigged head. "I love you, Melody," he said, "because you're such a little—little wishful hoper! Yes, 'wishful hoper,' that's the word for you. For the chance of Bill coming riding, striding, or any other way, into this show tonight, with or without any documents or documentary evidence or anything else, is equal to—can you take mathematics, honey?"

"Oh, yes, Jules. Exactly *how much* is the chance—you outline?"

"Exactly zero, honey," he laughed satisfiedly, "with the rim peeled off!"

CHAPTER XV

THE TRAVELLER

Bull Chattock, driving along the Foleysburg Road at firm speed, in the still generous light of early evening that preceded the dusk, and the grateful coolness that accompanied it, saw the circus front approaching him up ahead. Not due to any lights there, however, but because of the blaze of colour made by the particular trailers which, parked longitudinally there, created the "front."

Even the Big Top, visible back over the tops of the trailers, was a lightless black silhouette against the still bright sky, and the spires of the town, well back of everything, but glimpseable between the trailer roofs, were also silhouettes.

Now, because the dirt road on which Bill drove was firm and rutless, he was in front of the circus "front"—at least, in front of the midmost of the 5 trailers that fringed the right of the "gate."

The stout collapsible wooden latticework that formed "the gate," he could see, was drawn firmly across the 10-foot gap lying between the two huge vertical crimson-and-green striped posts affixed by clamps to the rear corners of the two trailers always used to create the "gate." All was so inordinately quiet that one might have thought there was going to be no circus, except that the usual number of youthful yokels, aged from 6 to 16, hickory-shirted most of them, lounged about fascinatedly on the grass across the road from the "front."

Now, from the great green-and-white chequered trailer—the largest of them all!—forming the very midmost of the 5 trailers fringing the right of "the gate," appeared a human being who, being occupant of this specific trailer, was none other than Angus MacWhorter, Proprietor of MacWhorter's Mammoth Motorized Shows, which right now were demonstrating a bewildering absence of pre-show activity.

Tall and even ganglingly broad as he was, he filled the entire doorway of the trailer, even though minus the tall silk hat and black frock-coat with which he always and invariably appeared in public; his great brooding long face, with the deep seams in it, and the high grey-touched sideburns each side, and the hair above it all thinning because of his 60 or so years of age, was beaming out instant welcome to the man on the road.

"Hi, Bill!" he called. "I recognized the vibration of your engine. Come in."

Bill Chattock, who had drawn to an immediate stop—a stop that would have been a skidding stop on anything but a dirt road—on sight of his superior, looked back from his high perch at the gleaming white square truck body forming his background.

"But Mr. Mac," he said questioningly, "I—"

"Yes, of course." And now MacWhorter put his great hands to his own mouth and called loudly—into nowhere:

"Baron? Baron?"

Almost as though by magic, there slithered out from under the trailer, having evidently come directly from the other side, a man, rubbing his eyes, plainly one who had been quietly having a snatch of sleep on the ground. As he clambered to his feet, he could be seen to be a Paris apache! At least, he wore the red-and-black striped jersey of one, and a cap that was pulled sinisterly far down over one eye; from his lips—the very corner thereof!—even drooped a cigarette—an unlighted cigarette—suggesting that he must have drawn it instanter from his pocket, and popped it into his mouth, thus completing his get-up.

"Yah, yah, Herr!" he cried, looking up toward MacWhorter. *"Vass villst du? Hab Ich dich gehört, aber—"*

"Stop your nonsense, Baron," said MacWhorter with a grimace. "A new one yet, eh? German. What in heaven's name don't you know or can't you do? Don't you realize the get-up you've got on right now is French, and not—take that truck yonder through the gate and in, and put it with the regular vehicles in the trailer lot."

"Oui-oui!" said Baron Munchausen, becoming a non-German instantly.

And he was hopping up on the truck seat even as Bill, thanks to having his blue serge coat on him instead of under him, was climbing down on the free side. And even as Bill was crossing over to MacWhorter's trailer, the white truck, containing a small matter of $3,000 in cash, was rumbling to the gate; its driver was dexterously reaching far out, over, and back of the top of the latticework, unlatching it somewhere, flinging it full wide open and back, and driving in. Hopping off, once inside by one truck-length, to fasten the gate again. And Bill, now at MacWhorter's trailer, and hearing the reassuring "Gang—way!" inside, knew at last that he had truly "brought the babe home."

MacWhorter was standing aside, holding open, with one giant tree-trunk of an arm, the trailer door. Bill stepped up and in. The gaunt cheerless interior of the trailer, made so because of its so few and so ascetic pieces of furniture, and its complete lack of colour, seemed not to have the same gauntness as usual. For MacWhorter's bunk, at one end, looked crumpled—at least, its black cover-lid was flung loosely up, as though it had been napped upon within but the last hour. Moreover, MacWhorter's huge Bible lay open, with a loose black ribbon marker atop it, on a portable table underneath the high small window on the lot side, letting in, however, plenty of light on its huge primer type, and revealing that the flapping black canvas back of MacWhorter's customary Bible-reading chair had at long last gone through. Since the chair was now—backless! And all of which—particularly the matter of the open Bible—was odd, too, since MacWhorter usually read his nightly chapter after the show was over.

"I've been reading my nightly chapter now," he explained to Bill, as he closed the door. Plainly getting Bill's surprised glance toward the huge open Bible. "Because it's been arranged that tonight after show-close—after, that is, the white truck would have been brought in by you—the bank is to officially take over all the money in the safe. And issue me—just in here, that is—the various cashier's cheques and all we'll need for salaries, bills—so forth. And, of course, to cash such salary cheques as our folks want to cash. And so," he finished sheepishly, "I'll be busier than a wet hen tonight after show-close. With the prosaic business of—banking! And probably, moreover, during all the time between show-close and pull-out hour. Well," he broke off, "glad you got here, boy. I was worried about you."

"About me?" asked Bill in surprise. "Why?"

MacWhorter's great face looked downright sheepish.

"You'll laugh, I'm afraid—when I tell you why! However, 'twas because—but sit here, boy, do. You've had *some* drive today."

He took from the only chair where perched, hung and stood respectively, the tall silk hat, the frock-coat which gave him that awesome dignity he always presented when he stepped into the ring, and the blackthorn cane, swinging the chair around to face his table, and taking the garments and cane over to the bunk, where he dropped them, and came back. The while Bill still stood.

"No, take it, boy. It's got a back. And you've had *some* drive. I'd much rather myself have that canvas-seated monstrosity yonder even if it now at last has no back! For the seat, thanks to the sag in it, sort of accommodates my—well, my underside. Take the chair, yes."

So Bill did take the chair. Disposing of his broad-brimmed grey felt hat that had been clear to Europe with him and back, by turning it over downward, and thrusting it smartly against the floor by his side, just enough to make it stand jauntily upright. MacWhorter, meanwhile, had turned his hammock-like canvas chair partly around—had settled down into it, facing Bill.

"And why," Bill now asked, ever so curiously, "did you feel worried about me?"

MacWhorter grimaced freely.

"Well, I'll tell you—but don't laugh at me, will you? I had a dream in which, by George, the white office-truck was a sort of mis-shapen sort of a bashed-about golf-ball, and you a giant golfer—trying to drive it, with a golf stick, across Idiot's Valley, along Old Twistibus. Rather, should I perhaps say, that you were normal enough in size, but that the Valley was sort of like—like a miniature golf-course. The Valley—the course through Old Twistibus—was nothing but a great multi-golf-hazard. There were weird sand-traps, water-traps, bottomless holes—red demons with mashies trying to drive *your* ball off the fairway. I said—in the dream, you understand, Bill—I said, 'No man can pass all those hazards. He may pass one—may pass another—but all—never! He can't drive the ball—across.' After which," said MacWhorter, waving his two huge hands about in the air, "I woke up, and sat down here, and opened up my Bible for the reading I'd intended anyway to do earlier today—and lo, heard down the road the vibration of an oncoming vehicle. And a few seconds later, recognized it definitely as our white office-truck motor."

Bill shook his head, half chidingly. "You really needn't have worried so. Of course, your knowledge of that three thousand dollars in that money-transporting safe was forcing its way through your consciousness—and causing you to make up a set-up in the dream quite the opposite to the one that really existed: one that we might call the 'everything on the q.t. and all quiet on the Western front!' That's the theory of dreams offered by a certain Russian philosopher chap called Ouspensky. Calls it 'Complementary tone' creation. Calls it—but here—do you mind telling me why everything is so quiet? Why—well, obviously it's due to a dislocation of our opening-hour—but what's it all about? Never before did I see things at this hour so gravelike."

"It's very simple, Bill," MacWhorter explained. "The Mayor asked me personally, after we got here, to open tonight at 8:30 instead of 7:30. I consented to the Mayor's wishes—gladly!—since he said 'twould be published in this afternoon's *Foleysburg Gazette,* and bulletined all over town—I consented by fixing for the platform and stroll-about stuff to cover only 30 minutes tonight, instead of an hour. You see, we're all sold out uptown, having no ticket selling problems now. So everybody in the outfit's just lolling around now, revelling in a period of ease they never customarily get at this hour. Soaking it in, as it were!"

"What on earth," asked Bill, "did the Mayor want our opening put back for?"

"Well, it seems, Bill," said MacWhorter, "that he's scheduled to give an address tonight in the square uptown from 7 to 8. At least, with the various embellishments to it. And has promised to announce in it something that, so he has claimed, that will be of interest to every man, woman and child—and get this, Bill!—unborn babe in Foley County. So he wanted to be able to announce just as he began speaking that the circus, two blocks south, wouldn't open a crack till 8:30—so's everybody wouldn't start to drift away later from his audience. For once they get his surprise bomb, they'll all start drifting."

"What on earth can his bombshell be going to be?"

"Oh," said MacWhorter, "that's an easy one to guess. In view of hints he sort of—of dropped to me. Or I guess he did! It's undoubtedly to tell the town that the action their mayor brought before the Supreme Court toward invalidating the old Foley County land-grant conditions, is successful. That, in short, he has it on unimpeachable inside info' that the Supreme Court is going to hand down a decision next week finding Old Man Foley's conditions invalid. Which would mean that any man in Foleysburg as well as all Foley County can now have a phone in his house—the town can have both phone and telegraph lines—that it may at last be a civilized city!"

"And," nodded Bill, "its mayor can thus be re-elected unanimously. However, I'll offer one now! It's this: maybe he's going to tell 'em the hard and sad news that the Supreme Court won't invalidate old Foley's grants—and that they therefore live in one of the most re-mark-a-ble villages in all America."

"Right!" said MacWhorter sepulchrally. "But whether he's going to crow—or commiserate—that's why we're opening late."

"Well," nodded Bill, "Jules won't object, I daresay, to doing a few fewer tricks than usual. And Harry can snake off his robe sooner, after a shorter spell, and flap it back on quicker. Just as Dollykins can—so your dream bothered you, eh, Chief?" he broke off.

"Bothered me? I'll say. I woke up sweating, I tell you, it was so real. So vivid."

Bill was studiedly thoughtful.

"You say I was a giant golfer—rather, an ordinary golfer looking down on a miniature Old Twistibus and Idiot's Valley?"

"Yes," nodded the elderly Scotchman. "At least that's the way I got it. Like it was a miniature golf-course—rather than that you were big. But, oh—the traps that were there! Sand-traps—water-traps—holes—even a mechanical tiger—sabre-toothed too, Bill, quite in line with that prehistoric region!—snarled and showed its teeth at one bend in Old Twistibus. And—well, I said, in my dream, there isn't a chance for that mis-shapen white ball—*my* truck!—to be bowled through. He can't make it!"

Bill now fell silent. For he'd heard other theories about dreams than the complementary tone theories of Ouspensky. That dreams were bits of reality—wildly combined, yes, but nevertheless real bits.

Some, no more than "stills," from the dreamer's own immediate future. Some, on the other hand, "stills" of the dreamer's many *possible* futures—his so-called "alternate actualizations" that lay poised in every second of his existence. Still others, seemingly clairvoyant as to Space and Time, being but part of other persons' actualizations connected to the dreamer's own. He shook his head. For he was neither philosopher, mystic, nor psychologist. He was just William T. Chattock, wine-chemist, bringing back to a much-loved sweetheart a simple birthday present that should—beyond all doubt would—in the case of her discouraged and downcast self, be greatly, greatly prized by her for all the rest of her life.

"Well, I got here okay, didn't I? So don't worry any more, Mr. MacWhorter. The truck never left my sight. The 3,000 dollars that were locked in it are still locked in it. It's all safe. Only, by golly, your dream—your dream *does* fascinate me. Because—"

He said no more. And it was MacWhorter who changed the subject.

"Well, all dreams aside, what did you think of Old Twistibus, boy?"

"The most amazing piece of natural roadway," said Bill promptly, and truthfully, "I've ever seen—in all my life. Whoever laid that out—but it's an old trail, evolved into a road, isn't it? For—say, at some points, so help me, a person crossing the Valley westward is actually going east."

"I know!" chuckled MacWhorter. "How I know! Heavens, Bill, haven't I brought the show across the valley by Old Twistibus a dozen times, over the last 12 years? Did you have any odd or out-of-the-way experiences along Old Twistibus? With the people along it, I mean?"

"Nothing," said Bill, though a bit enigmatically, "to write a book about."

"What did you think," MacWhorter asked, "of that great swamp?"

"Oh, boy!" said Bill. Adding, quite truthfully: 'That is certainly the most lethal piece of green water I've ever viewed in my life. And—but that red roadway crossing it like a plank—becoming finally a grey road again as it sweeps up and out of the valley and into the Foleysburg Road—now that red roadway—is that something artificial? If so, how—"

"No, oh, no," MacWhorter informed him. "It's an upturned stratum face—merely levelled down, decades ago, by the army, to enable settlers-to-be to clamber out of that trap. Actually, Bill, it's two swamps, one on each side."

"Hm? Wonder if one ever osmoses across the barrier into the other?" This was the chemist speaking. And the chemist proceeded to speak as a chemist. "'Twould be interesting to measure the static pressures each side of that 'solution-separating medium.' And find—" He stopped with a smile.

How long," now asked MacWhorter eagerly, "did it take you—travelling out of train as *you* were—to cover Old Twistibus? It's said, you know, to be all of 140 miles in length with its twists and bends and loops comprising a valley which a bird could take in 80 miles straight—*if* he didn't fall dead. How long did it take you to get from one end of the valley to the other?"

"Oh—31 minutes, I guess!" said Bill quizzically.

"And now," smiled MacWhorter tolerantly, "we've got two Baron Munchausens on the outfit! All right then. Now, Baron—Baron No. I—is always best on the uptake. We'll see how you are, Baron No. II. Well, how'd you cross? Sprout 200-foot-long wings out of the truck—and fly? Or did a mammoth prehistoric eagle, who'd matured for thousands of years back in that valley, just carry you and that truck across in one of his claws?"

"Both of those solutions aren't far from the truth," said Bill gravely. "For the truck and I, Mr. MacWhorter, covered Idiot's Valley, east to west, this fateful day of Friday the 13th of June, in Uncle Sam's little-known secret weapon No. 31-*a*. Otherwise known as—Supercopter!"

MacWhorter gazed at his friend and helper as one not knowing whether to smile complacently at a good Munchausian yarn, or to frown at mere levity.

"Of course," he said, doing neither, "you're joking."

"No," said Bill.

"You—you really mean that—oh, Bill, you're doing a Munchausen, of course, aren't you? Why—that weapon doesn't even exist."

"Yes, it exists, Mr. MacWhorter. It's even able to swing 6 tanks from one battlefield, over hopeless terrain—and land them all on another battlefield. Why not? Carrying out constant maneuvers as it does, there on that lonely experimental ground in Central Texas?"

"Central—Texas? Good heav—well—ah—uh—what was it doing 'way up here north at Idiot's Valley? Bill, I'm sunk," groaned MacWhorter. "I don't know what this is all about. How—"

"You hardly could, Chief," conceded Bill. "For it happened this way. It all might be said to have started during the advance into France, on D-Day II. And revolves about—about a downed Allied airman named Gunlock Lanternman. Captain Gunlock Lanternman, and myself, plain infantryman. He—he always thought—thinks today, confound him!—that he would have been a dead pilot that day if he hadn't been yanked out of that burning plane, by someone who—who merely strolled across an open area and toted him back across it to behind a—oh, heck, he'd have crawled out by himself okay. In fact," he changed the subject quickly, "let's jump out of them hectic days to present time. During which period Cap'n Gunlock Lanternman has become Chief in charge of Special Helicopter Operations. Today he's in charge of that giant helicopter that Uncle Sam never even got completed during the war, in time to try out. I've heard from Gunlock a dozen times, there in Wine City. Always asking me, 'What *can* I do for you, old man? When can I return—You see," Bill complained, "the idiot has an—an *idée fixe, I* think the French call it—thinks I saved his fool life double that day he fell—from flame *and* bullets. And so has been at me—for years. To find out what he can do in return. The refrain always runs: 'Damn you, Chattock, what *can* I do?—if *ever* I can do something for you, tell me.'

"Oh—oh!" nodded MacWhorter, though not seeing at all. "And because today was the 13th and a Friday, you suddenly took a notion to—you mean," he said, but chidingly, "that, superstitious, you phoned 'way down to Texas—and asked him to—to—"

"Chief," put in Bill, "after I got done paying those good folks, the Elums, at the east tip of the Valley, not just a 10 per cent commission on two long phone calls but a 20 per cent one—you see, I'd called a chap in Wine City to check for me as to a certain pawn-ticket being valid—later, he rang me back, reversed the charges, of course, and told me everything was okay— well, after I got done paying the Elums the fattest phone commission they ever got in their lives, the poor wretches, they—they sort of took down their hair—with me. Told me that this morning when the show went by early, and stopped for distribution of coffee to the drivers, that a wax-moustached fellow in a crimson dressing-gown with gold stripes, out of one of the trailers, and buying some tobacco, asked them all sorts of questions about how far money went, down in the Valley. How the people down there were—with respect to their mazuma needs. Whether they were a—a ruthless sort of folk. How they could use mazuma, *if* they had any."

"Oh-oh!" nodded MacWhorter, frowning. "And you knew DiValo— doesn't smoke nor use tobacco?"

"That's right," nodded Bill. "And the two facts—that plus the specific angle and trend of his questions—showed *me* that beyond peradventure he was figuring to block me there in the valley today. By the use of mazuma. How seriously or how—how not seriously, I couldn't guess. But blocked I'd be, I was certain. For—well, I'm fetching some—some dope for Melody. Something—ah—registrational. Something that would affect a certain suit for her hand by said wax-moustached rat."

Bill stopped. Figuring he had gone too far with respect to one of his chief's employees.

"Go on, Bill?" said MacWhorter soothingly. "I knew there was rivalry between you. But I never interfered. I'm for the best man winning—the girl always choosing."

"I know that, Chief. Well, when I heard all that stuff from the Elums, I knew that with all the stops the show would have to make along that road— to permit gaps in it to close up—to change tyres—change wheels, distribute coffee and food—well, I haven't gone over these godawful long treks with you for nothing, you know! Well, I knew that Jules, during some of those stops, would fix up something with one of those hillbilly-mountaineer families that would insure that a certain little old me, following 9 hours or so later with a white truck, would never get through. It's life or death for him, in a manner of speaking, that I didn't get through today. Because if I didn't, Melody would be convinced that I had purposely hung back, because I'd failed at something vital for her—oh, he'd have sold her on some of the finer details of all this—the point is that she was about to throw in her lot with him, at—at show-close tonight, believing herself to be, poor child, something that she wasn't—sounds like colour-line stuff, doesn't it?—well, let it sound as it sounds. I cursed myself that I hadn't phoned in from the north to you to tell Melody that I had with me—*what* I did have. But—I hadn't! I was trapped, since the show was now in a town to which telephone service from outside, *and* telegraph service, were non-existent. I—Mr. MacWhorter, call me, if you want to, a nerve-wracked old woman, but I figured I was a gone cuckoo if I went through."

"No," said Angus MacWhorter tolerantly, "I won't. You are you—somebody else is somebody else—and I am me. What you uncovered there at Elum's probably wouldn't have upset me at all. I'd have just figured that—but you're in love, you see. But go on with your tale. I take it then, that, in a blue funk—quite unjustified, I believe—you rang clear across country to Texas. To this experimental ground?"

"That's what I did," retorted Bill. "I rang Lanternman himself, and told him briefly of the curious set-up I was up ag'in. And that I *was* calling for help now—at last! He had me outline carefully, by the towns around there, the two roads that I was virtually at the confluence of—you know, the Cedarville Road—and Carthage Road East?—and to locate the confluence with respect to the river—yes, I had to call on the Elums right there for distances and so forth—but once Gunlock had the locations, he had all he needed. He said, 'You stick there now whatever you do—don't you budge off the segment, no matter what happens—and I'll come for you. I'll not let you down. I'll come for you as sure as—as there are Uranium Atomic Bombs. I'll put you at that circus at Foleysburg *not* at show-close—not at dark—but definitely before both. Stick, damn you—stick!' Those," apologized Bill, with a glance at the Bible at MacWhorter's elbow, "were *his* words, not mine."

MacWhorter smiled reassurance.

"So-o-o," Bill continued the story, "there I stuck. All afternoon. I even had a small business date down in the valley—5 miles or so in—some friendly hillbilly had some wine his maw had made—I'd arranged to stop by there, at some woman novelist's lonely house, and taste it—see if I could help him locate the ingredients. But—no dice! For if that giant of the skies came while I was gone, where would I be? Right! Left at the post—one helicopter wheeling back towards Texas—its engineer-pilot named Lanternman figuring I was a louse of the first water—else one who'd decided, after all, to take it awheel through Old Twistibus. Stick—I did. Well, I was getting discouraged about the time that old red sun commenced to drift lower and lower toward that old horizon, but at last, when, as they say, all hope was lost—a curious speck appeared far to the southwest.

"At first I thought 'twas an eagle, mocking me. But it got—bigger and bigger. As it came close and closer on. Very soon the individual rotors could be seen—as on a toy. And the curious gleaming aluminum car that underhung the thing. It just came lower and lower as though being let down by invisible cables from the sky above. And the way," he now added, shaking his head, "that that trained crew, in red-trimmed grey uniforms, swarmed out of the—the cab—and down upon rope ladders that were flung out-well, they lashed the great padded hooks of the left frontmost set of claws or tank-holders, or whatever you call 'em, together under the truck some way, and before I'd hardly had a chance to say, 'Hello—you old sun of a gun'—the crew members were swarming back up and in—we were off—before I had my breath."

"And they put you and the truck down," helped out MacWhorter, though puzzledly, "on that other plateau—Simpson's Junction—where the Valley road comes up out, and joins the Foleysburg Road."

"He was going to first," offered Bill. "But then he thought, travelling at the speed he could with those pusher-propellers, that he ought to cut some real time off of my haul. By descending closer to my destination. But not— not to go anywheres close to the circus here, and spoil your show with the Foleysburg people."

"That—that was darned decent of him," granted Angus MacWhorter. "A giant bird like that, seen from town this evening, would have put a crimp into our 'caravan of wonders.'"

"That's what Gunlock himself averred," admitted Bill. "So he tacked sort of diagonally across the northern expanse of that swamp, and cut the Foleysburg Road at a point he computed was about an hour off from Foleysburg. Directly above that white thread of a road we stopped—hovered there in space— lower, lower, lower, we descended vertically—till some light on the instrument board showed that the lowered contact had presumably touched ground. Out swarmed the men. A couple of signals lowered the gargantuan thing to set the truck wheels squarely on the ground, the holding-devices under and about the truck an' all, were unlocked, unlatched, unbuckled—whatever you want to term it—the men were swarming back up and—off went the thing. Vanishing away in the southwest, a speck!—then, so help me, a dream. That's right, Mr. MacWhorter! When I found myself sitting in the seat of the truck there in Foleysburg Road, all alone, rubbing my eyes from having been looking at the sky, and no more than 30 miles out from here, I—I wondered if I'd dreamed it all. And perhaps had actually driven through Old Twistibus in some kind of a cataleptic trance. Instead of—of having been a jittery old woman having done that—that—that test-tube baby a great injustice."

"What—what did I hear you say? Test-tube-baby?"

"Jules has a clipping about himself showing him to have been—been born in a Paris clinic by—by artificial insemination—you know?—experiment in eugenics—"

"Oh—fiddle!" snorted MacWhorter. "What nonsense. I have some papers of his and a passport that he took out only six months ago, apparently to go abroad. He—well, you see, Bill, he brought a kid out of the Valley today. He plainly promised to make the kid his helper, though I'm personally confident his idea is to get a free valet, lackey, and errand-boy, and whatnot out of the kid. For—anyway, he left the kid alone in his trailer early this afternoon; and the kid, seeing this passport and folder, with papers in it, sticking out from under his pillow-case, filched it! Anyway, Silver-Tongue found the kid wandering about the lot, and brought him in here to me at once. Where, of course, when he tightened up as to exactly who he was and how he happened to be here, I searched him—and took the passport and papers from him. For— however, the point I'm trying to get at is that the passport and papers show that DiValo's real name is Snopczinski—yes, he's a blond Pole—his name is Czeslaw Snopczinski, though don't try to spell it!—he was born in Milwaukee, the 14th of 21 children granted by a somewhat generous Fate to an obviously good Polish Catholic woman named Irena Snopczinski."

"The—the hell you say, Chief! I—excuse my Anglo-Saxon, Chief. The deuce you say? Born via proper wedlock, eh? Test-tube baby—is good."

"Odd," mused MacWhorter, "that he'd want to claim that. Baron would be jealous as all get-out, if he ever heard that invention."

"Not odd, Chief," offered Bill, "when you know the facts."

"What on earth do you mean, Bill?"

"It's a long story, Chief," Bill replied, and arose. "All I can say at this juncture is that the most puffect Act II in all history is now ready to be played out! Properly, I mean! As per the best theatrical traditions. For not only has the He-ro brought home the cancelled mortgage—or just as good!—but the villain—ah, the villain is!—if he can only be decoyed on to the stage, is in full position to be unfrocked. Unfrocked, as he stands before the her-o-ine—twirling his very moustaches. And saying 'Curse you all!' For—but I'll just bob on now, Chief, if you don't mind; and see you later. For—what's that? What on earth *is* this all about? Oh, nothing much. Just that Papa has brought home the bacon. The marines have arrived. And now for Melody."

CHAPTER XVI

"OVER THE WALL AND AT 'EM, BOYS!"

Bill, standing in front of the scarlet-and-green striped trailer realized disgruntledly that the marines had landed—but to an empty house! For to his jovial cry against the partly-open trailer door of "Hi, an'body home in there?" there was but the starkest of silence.

"Well," he said disgruntledly to himself, as he stepped up, and shoved on the broad pivoted door, "I can write out a message with lipstick, on her dressing-table mirror."

But as he stepped into the trailer, an odd sight met his eyes. For Melody, in her little puff-sleeved, low-throated, green velvet walk-about-grounds dress, sat on her light dressing-table chair, her hand on her heart, her face gone white, her red lips actually open as though in some kind of astonishment.

Diagonally across the available open space in the trailer, next the door-side end of the meshwork cutting off the paraphernalia, on a low stool, sat a strange comical figure in hugely-chequered loose clothing, a sad black eye, a long red-tipped paper nose that looked exactly like a flesh-and-blood one, an unkempt fringe of red hair about its artificially-bald head, atop which, though far to one side, perched a small cup-sized brown derby hat. And the figure's mouth—at least such of it as could be seen between the bows of the huge drooping moustache—was wide open, too.

"Bill!"

It was Melody who had given utterance to the cry. Indeed, she was on her feet, and colour had flooded back to her face.

"Hy-ya, darling," he said casually, jauntily sailing his hat dexterously up atop the edge of the upper bunk. "Hy-ya, mister," he added, to the individual on the stool. "Newcomer, eh, to the outfi—for the—the luvva Mike—the villain! The villain—himself!"

The adam's apple of the villain moved visibly, but no words came from his lips.

"Well, darling," Bill said, turning back to the girl, "I'm back—as you can see."

He stepped over to her, and kissed her, full on her lips.

"Glad—to see me?"

Now she found words. "Oh, Bill! Always—always glad to see you—of course. And so you hitchhiked on—to at least tell me in person—that you failed? Well, I knew you had."

"What's 'at?" he said sharply. "Failed? Hitchhiked on? To—what do you mean, darling?"

"Why, I mean, Bill, from that point in the woods, along the Foleysburg Road, where you talked to Harry, early this morning. After flying down here—from Detroit. Where—"

"Talked—to Harry? Flew down—from Detroit?" He looked about the trailer at the curious figure sitting there. Then back to the girl.

"Listen, darling. I don't know what on earth's been told you—around this outfit. But I just came through the Valley. Over Old Twistibus."

"But, Bill," she expostulated. "You never came down to Pricetown."

Bill turned to the figure on the stool again. It raised sheepish hands, palms outward, in a queer gesture.

"Don't ask me, Melody," it said, but solely in the direction of the girl. "All I know—is what you do. What Harry told us. Ask Harry—when he comes back."

Bill turned his gaze to the girl. She looked about to faint. He stepped forward, and pressed her gently, but firmly, back into her chair.

"Now—now let's get to the bottom of this," he said sternly. "Harry—Harry's told you some wild story, all right, if it's about me being in the bushes. No, I've come from Pricetown. Brought the white office-truck with me. And, darling—hold on to your chair now—this is my great day. Darling, I found out your folks were married—by bell, book and candle!"

"Married? Oh, Bill! You—you fight to the end, don't you?—to at least make me feel happy? But, dear Bill—"

"Don't believe any fakealoo, honey," said the villain, over on the stool. "You're going to hear puh-lenty, from now on. You—"

"Yeah?" said Bill. "Listen, you wax-moustached—ah—you paper-nosed—oh, skip it—this is the—the damn'dest landing of the marines I ever saw— ever'time I want to do my big speech, I see a confounded monstrosity squatted on a stool, with a pea of a derby hat on one side of his bald—skip it. Darling—" He turned his head back toward the girl, and said no more, but withdrew from his breast pocket a folded paper.

"Listen, darling," he now said, "this is going to sound really crazy to you. But I've been clear to London since I saw you last. I found the Beowulf. No, not there. Back here in America. I found the line in it. Found the town—in the line. Found—but gaze on this. This is a photostat of the marriage-register page in the church rectory of the town where your daddy and mother were married—married by all the legal and ecclesiastical rites anybody could ever ask for."

And rising sufficiently from his bunk-edge seat, to extend it to her, he passed it over. She took it, gingerly, unbelievingly. And now the villain spoke up.

"Melody, don't believe a word of it! Photostats prove nothing. Ever! You can paste a slip of paper over—over another paper, and photograph both together—he could have bought a church-registry page from some old book, forged signatures on it—photostats aren't even evidence in law."

The girl had been gazing at the photostat in wonderment. Now she looked up, but in Jules's direction.

"Jules, this is Mother's own handwriting. Her handwriting—of which Bill knew absolutely nothing. And it's also Father's, of course. But as to Mother's signature, it's got her strange unmistakable M—her most peculiar S—her way of making the cross of the 't' in 'Smith' become the 'h.' Nobody on earth knew Mother's handwriting, as I've kept my lone two specimens home in a trunk."

She looked now toward Bill Chattock. Her face literally beamed.

"Well," he inquired genially, "did Papa bring home the bacon?"

"Oh, Bill!" she cried. "Bacon!—Did you bring home the—oh, Bill, you— you brang home—the whole hawg!"

Bill frowned. He had never heard this line, from lips of fair lady, in all the riverboat dramas he'd seen in his entire life. "You brang home the whole hawg." Hm? But her voice—the supreme tenderness radiating from it—that *was* always in the voice of the heroine when she took from the fingers of the returning hero the cancelled mortgage.

But now she had turned eyes on Jules DiValo. They were compassionate eyes, however, eyes radiating tenderness and sympathy.

"Poor Jules!" she said. "It had to happen—because it was in the Plan of Things to happen. I always told you, Jules, remember, that it was Bill I loved—that I was marrying you only because we were illegitimate—both. But now this—oh, I'm only so sorry now for you, Jules. That you must go through life now by yourself—from the point of legitimacy."

"What's 'at?" said the hero. Except that it must be admitted he howled it. "Melody, MacWhorter has a passport of Jules, and some papers, filched by a hillbilly kid he fetched through. His—Jules, I mean-name is Coldslaw Sloppypinupapee—he was born in Milwaukee—the—the 27th child of a woman named Wheatena—no, Irena—and a father named Henryowicz—he was baptized in a church bigger than the Chicago Stadium."

Mr. Czeslaw Snopczinski had arisen.

"This," he said dignifiedly, "is where I came in."

He strode across the bit of open space in the trailer, heaved the door far enough open to drop down to the ground outside, looked up and in.

"S'long, Melody," he said. "I'm digging out of the outfit—yes, now—soon's I can get over to the P.O. and the mail auto, stripping off this get-up on the way." He gazed up at Bill. A gaze which Bill, from his long early experience with melodrama, knew was the most ferocious gaze in all the world. A gaze of venom, of defeat. A gaze which said "Curse you, Chattock, curse you!" Except that all Bill could see was a pathetic comic figure with a pea of a hat far askew on a bald head—one sad black eye—a nose as long as one's hand. "You can't blame me for trying, can you?" he said mildly, and was gone.

And the hero and heroine were left alone.

"My God, darling," Bill said, "what—what an Act II! The marines spring over the wall with the cancelled mortgage—the heroine tells the hero he brang home—yes, brang home the whole hawg!—the villain wobbles off, dressed exactly like the comic in a 4th-rate burlesque show—but oh—oh—unkindest cut of all!—oh, worst technical *faux pas* in history, by Fate the Dramatist—oh, lousiest Act II of all Act II's—"

"What, Bill? What is so wrong—when we—we have come together at last happily?"

"The villain," he said grumpily, "never even once said—bah!"

CHAPTER XVII

CONCERNING THE MURDER OF A BLACK RAGPICKER

Bill, lolling comfortably in the special chair of the professional fat woman, which was virtually a settee, the slim little green-velvet-clad form seated on its edge by him, facing him, though just now atop his chest and tight in his arms, listened gravely as she spoke.

"But, Bill, how—how can you ever want now to marry a girl who was willing to marry another man, when she—"

"Pish, tush, and a couple of tiddles on that," he said. "Believing you were illegitimate"—he flung his gaze sidewise; saw that the trailer door was, this time, shut—"certainly took *you*—for a ride. But that's—the difference atween people! With you, poor kid, it was the end of the world. All you could think of was to live out your life in the safe company of a man worse off than yourself."

"Why, Bill! You're—you're saying the identical thing the villain's supposed to say. What is this—anyway?"

"Heaven knows," he laughed. "But no—as to not wanting to marry you, I mean. Whatever else, I do understand how that phony belief—knocked you out. Now *me,* I wouldn't give two whoops. If I were illegitimate, I'd say—to hell with it! I'd marry, under such conditions, and freely, a girl whose folks had been married by bell, book and candle—bridesmaids and best men— flower-girls—and archbishops!—I'd tell her who and what I was."

"And see her, some fine day," the girl said, now seated upright, "surveying you critically."

"I understand," he returned. "Well, Pappy got here all right. Brang with him the whole hawg—zowie! Brang—anyway, Jules is out. And as for Harry—well, we'll have to wait for his return to see whether Jules had something on him, and—if he did, then Jules plainly rigged something up ag'in me, down there in the Valley—we'll have to find out that more or less by indirection, by finding out whether Harry'd been smoking marijuana cigarettes—when he spouted all that stuff. 'Bout *me*—being in the bushes on the Foleysburg Road. Probably the latter is true enough. And—best, however, to say nothing to Harry, I guess." She leaned forward, put a soft cheek against his own.

"How glad I am," she said fervently, "that you did get here all right. Did anything at all happen along Old Twistibus that might have suggested that Jules—in short, did you have an uneventful journey across the Valley?"

"Hah!" he said. "And there's also one—out of mellerdrammer. Yea, hah! You got lots to learn, about the journey across the Valley. You—but it can wait. Just now I want to sort of squeeze you a lot, to make up for all the squeezing I've wanted to give you—the while I've been branging home the whole hawg."

"It's—it's been a nightmare," the girl said gravely. "And I—want to forget it. I never could have believed it of Aunt Olivia, though. Her letting me believe I was—well, I almost believe now that she may have been—in love with my father."

"Could be, easily," he admitted. "Perversion of a sort, you know."

She lay silent against him a moment, emotionally exhausted.

"But, Bill—"

"Yep, darling? What?"

"Since Papa's story about the church-rectory marriage-register page *was* correct, then I take it that it did carry, on its back, in code, and code only, the inside story of that Ragpicker Joe Murder? Or at least, in case you weren't able to decode it all, something we can presume is that?"

"Oh, yes, yes." Bill nodded hastily. "Naturally it was there, since the page itself proved to exist. I had that side of the register-page photostated too-worked on it, on the way from Floyd to Cincinnati. With your father's little Codoscope device. Which—oh, by the way—He felt around into his side coat pocket for the thing she wanted returned, reached it with his fingers, and drew it out. "There 'tis," he said. "A memento of your own father that you wrote specifically must—*must!*—be returned!"

"Thank you so much," she said, and dropped it in an outer pocket of her dress. "You see," she explained, "I—I want some day to go to Floyd myself—just to see Mama's and Papa's writing in their own ink."

"And," he put in quizzically, "you'll so much want to see his exact phraseology, in his little recorded story on the back, that you'll work that out too?"

"Good heavens!" she exclaimed. "I wouldn't know—where to begin."

"Oh, yes, you would," he corrected. "For when I confronted the photostat, on the train going from Floyd to Cincinnati, I—but let's put *you* in front of the page. No, I haven't the photostat now. Having written in letters aplenty over the code lines, I—I just tore it up. But here! Suppose you were—will be, eventually, say—confronting the mess of jumbled letters, spaced off into obvious words, in your father's coded recordment? Yea, I know there's no such word as 'recordment,' but I kind of like it myself! I—well, now what, of all the words in the English language, could you be sure would be in that particular messa—ah—recordment?"

"Why—uh—well, 'Ragpicker Joe Murder.' Somewhere."

"Of course!" he assented. "So you would run along the huddles that comprised putative words, till you found—"

"Of course! Yes. Found three, in sequence, that contained—let's see?— 9 and—and 3—and 6 letters?"

"Right," he nodded. "And then—what would you do? I mean—with the Codoscope in hand?"

"Well, I'd—I'd probably," she ventured, "set the J of the inner revolving alphabet—the true alphabet!—against the first letter of that 3-letter jumbled word, as found in the outer scrambled, or code-alphabet, just to see if—"

"Yes?"

"—to see," she went on thoughtfully, "if the O and the E also on the inner alphabet were against the same letters in the code-alphabet as—as recorded in the three-letter code word."

"Exactly," he declared. And nodded. "Which in my case they proved to be. Showing the coded word was 'Joe.'"

"But now comes the fun!" She nodded. "For the ingeniousness of Father's device was—is based on the ability of a coder to slide that revolving inner alphabet ever, ever ahead—or back—after *any kind of a mathematical system*. For otherwise those—those numerically calibrated red circles on each disc wouldn't have been there. So assuming, as is most likely, that the dials were changed *every* time a word was coded—"

"What more do you want, gal," he demanded, "on a curve—but three points? I mean—well, suppose you had tried out, now, for the word 'Ragpicker'—the word in front of the confirmed one, 'Joe,' and it would definitely be 'Ragpicker'—and in order to get the jumbled letters found in its coded form alongside the alphabetical letters forming *it*, you had to—to move the inner revolving disc back by 3 places? What would you think?"

"We-ell," she returned dubiously, "I'd—I'd only know that to get from 'Ragpicker' to 'Joe' there'd been one advance setting of 3 numbers. Or places. But—but, of course, you checked then for 'Murder,' and found—well, what did you find, Bill?"

"Found," he said, "that the next setting of the dial had been by an advance of 5 places."

"Hm?" she mused. "Could have been a system where the last 2 numbers in the series kept ever adding up—like, say, 1, 2, 3, 5, 8, 13—"

"Could have been a million systems," he admitted. Only—the next following word was one of three letters. Now if it were 'was,' then—well, it checked as at least having a setting giving 'was,' and which setting was—7 places advanced."

"Oh," she cried, "3, 5, 7? Then—then the system of change might have been—was, that is—1, 3, 5, 7, 9, 11, 13 and so on ever upward?"

"Whoa, Tilley!" he said. "If it hadn't started over somewhere, your father would have had to spend his life just revolving dials and counting revolutions as well as spaces! And I doing the same—decoding it. No, fortunately it starts over again after it gets settings advanced with respect to each other by 1, 3, 5, 7, 9 and 11 places. Starts over—with the same sequence. And all of which means that the message can't ever be decoded by any outsider. For one has to have two vital things in order to decode it. One, the knowledge of *what* the message is about. The other—the Codoscope itself!"

"And you decoded it?" she said.

"Easy," was his answer. "The hardest thing of all, probably, was the locating of the code letters in that scrambled outer alphabet! Though after looking up about 20 in it, I got so used to that particular alphabet that I could find letters in it easier than I can find A in the true alphabet. No fooling! No, all I had to do was to keep shoving the rotating dial forward, at each word found, by 1, 3, 5, 7, 9 and 11 places—and then all over again. And the whole inside story of the Ragpicker Joe Murder was there—beautifully condensed, of course, as to the unnecessary 'the's' and 'a's'—and unnecessary adjectives and adverbs and all that. Sort of in—in a precis, you might call it. But, like a message in precis, it can be expanded right back into English, particularly when you've read the crime-story-magazine story of the Ragpicker Joe Murder. Have you?"

She nodded. "And how!"

"And I," he admitted.

"Can I—I see some of the pieces of the photostat?" she asked eagerly.

"Alas," he told her, "I burned them up, every one, when I got to Cincinnati."

"Why, Bill? Why?"

"Well, I might have lost them somewhere. Some curiosity seeker might have found them—enough to put same together—and send the whole to the police. They'd have gotten around to you via the name Ashbrooke, and from running down other names in it. True, all the parties involved in it are dead today. All, that is, but one. For I checked by long-distance phone in Cincinnati. It revealed, yes, that all are dead but one today. That one being—right!—the murderer in the case. One of the principal parties in it—a woman —the only woman in the case, in fact—dropped dead only 6 days ago, in a drug store in New Orleans, where she'd gone to have some kind of a heart operation. The surgeon who was to have operated read about the dropping dead in the newspapers, went to the morgue, and identified her. And that's how the police of her home city got to know what happened—down in New Orleans. And which was how *I* got the facts of the dropping dead, for your father's recordment gave her home city as Des Moines, Iowa. And it was to the police of Des Moines that I phoned for information on her. And—but you do want the explanation, don't you, darling, of that old murder?"

The girl nodded. "Naturally," she answered, "my curiosity has become great, about that."

"And will become greater," he said, "as time goes on—since your own father knew the facts. With the result that you'll go to Floyd yourself some day—spin dials—okay, then." He paused. "Well, here, then," he said, "amplified from his precis-like recordment back to—to straight narrative, is the full inside story of the killing of Ragpicker Joe—and his deposit, as you might put it, within the precincts of a quaint old hotel in Chicago called the Hotel Romanorum, with an Ace of Spades impaled on his unwashed back by a $25,000 jewelled dagger. Okay, darling—here goes!"

* * * *

"The story centers," began Bill Chattock reflectively, "about one, Luke Vaneau, an unsuccessful burlesque-show comedian playing, a quarter-century back, in third-rate burlesque in a small Minneapolis theatre. Your father underlined the word 'unsuccessful'—adding only the descriptive explanation that Luke Vaneau was apparently a sort of a morose individual to boot. But the whole combination, darling, presents the whole picture of Vaneau. Playing with him in this third-rate company was his wife, Mabrue. A beautiful, golden-haired creature—"

"The woman in the case," the girl nodded. "The—the Goldie, I mean? Who eventually confided in Father the real facts of that case. He said—he said that Goldie was intimately connected with the events—and all the persons in it—that's the Goldie who was the source of all this, isn't it, Bill?"

"I fear," Bill said dryly, "that I make things too easy—by introducing the golden-haired member of the case right after the main actor, and—but—back to our muttons. There's lots to follow. Luke Vaneau discovered, there in Minneapolis, that his beautiful wife, Mabrue—who incidentally had come of a fine family, but was secretly playing in cheap burlesque—had become mixed up, back in Louisville, Kentucky, where they'd played some weeks before, with a wealthy idler named—well, he was, at least by blood, half-Russian and half-German; his mother had named him after her father, one Asoff Korislov, and his father, having been a wealthy hides-dealer named Rudolph Spaetz—"

"Why," put in the girl, "then—then he was named—Asoff Spaetz? I am beginning to see darkly—heavens, I see nothing at all yet. Nothing at all!"

"Hardly, darling, hardly!" laughed Bill Chattock. "But back to our muttons again. Spaetz was hopelessly infatuated with Luke Vaneau's beautiful wife Mabrue, and had secretly given her a valuable jewelled dagger that he, Spaetz, had picked up in Vienna or somewhere during the course of a playboy tour he made of Europe right after World War I, then lying only a quarter-dozen or so years back of the events I'm relating. The jeweller he got it from had died the day after he bought it, and had himself picked it up in the distress market that filled Europe after that war—or even acquired it perhaps years before, as a stolen item. That's why it never became identified in the case I'm about to relate. Never—but Spaetz gave this beautiful item to Mabrue to prove to her he truly meant business with respect to his love. Would marry her and all that, you know? And it was Vaneau's finding of this valuable trinket in Mabrue's things that tipped him off—made him put pressure on her—extract a confession from her.

"He was beside himself, of course, with jealous rage. Quite unknown to his wife, he called Spaetz up, by long-distance, and asked to have a talk with him about divorce from Mabrue and 'financial terms' thereto. Asked Spaetz to come to some convenient point between Louisville and Minneapolis. And Spaetz, it seems, jumped at the chance to get Vaneau's wife through such a simple means as money—for money was the one thing that was absolutely no problem to him. Chicago was fixed on, naturally enough, as the most convenient point between the two cities, for this—this business meeting, as you might term it. Spaetz, unfamiliar with Chicago himself, strangely, asked Vaneau where they should hold their meeting; and Vaneau, who had stayed once or twice at the Hotel Romanorum in Chicago, because of its being a theatrical hotel, and him being in show-business himself—indeed, he'd stayed there so late as but one year before—well, he named that, as a logical place. Told Spaetz to register there, on the day agreed upon, and that he himself would call Spaetz there, by phone, when he got to Chicago, for a more specific appointment.

"To all of which," said Bill reflectively, "Spaetz greedily assented—was evidently quite confident he was going to buy this golden-haired beauty very, very cheap!—told Vaneau he would register there under the name of Alexander Brown. And thus terminated—the initial and preliminary arrangements. Vaneau arrived in Chicago in the evening of the day in question, called up the Hotel Romanorum, and found that Spaetz was there, all right, under the name Alexander Brown. Spaetz was, he told Vaneau, in Room 11, on the second floor. At the head of the stairway, he said, and facing same. Told Vaneau just to walk right in, in case he, Spaetz, wasn't there at the moment, as was likely to be the case, he said."

"But Luke Vaneau, I take it," the girl put in, though quite puzzledly, "intended perhaps to kill Spaetz? And not even to talk over *any* deal about the—the veritable sale of his own wife?"

"Precisely!" nodded Bill. "The very effrontery—the contumely—of the idea in Spaetz's head literally burned Vaneau up. He loved his wife fiercely, I gather from your father's notes. He—of course, after all the events I am about to relate were over with, only divorce was possible. Divorce—and an assignment to her of part of some small inheritance of $3,000 Vaneau was eventually to get from some grandfather. But that night all Vaneau could hold in his mind was his intention to kill Spaetz and flee. Foregoing, as a fugitive about the earth, his inheritance of that $3,000 and all. Yes, he intended to kill Spaetz—with the actual 'dagger of treachery.' So that if Mabrue heard the news before, say, he was able to contact her by phone or in person or somehow, and tell her grimly *what* he'd done, *how,* and *why,* she would know exactly what *she'd* done—by accepting that trinket. Vaneau, moreover, carrying the weapon in a little loose canvas bag, had even spitted on to it tightly, face towards the hilt, an Ace of Spades for the reason, as became conveyed later to your father, that this wealthy playboy was well known, at least down there in his own city of racehorses, and blue-bloods, and would thus be swiftly identified, despite his pseudonym used up in Chicago, by at least the reporters there in Louisville, who'd glean, from the spitted card, that it was identification of some sort—would tentatively put it together—'Ace of Spades'— 'Asoff Spaetz'—would check, by phone, Mr. Playboy—find he was *non est* there in Louisville—and would know, one and all, that he'd been estopped this time from wandering into the sacred precincts of other men's wives—oh, the motivating of jealousy-crazed persons, Melody, is always a bit—well—phrenetic. Well, at close on to 10:30 that night, 10:30 being the hour for the appointment for the talk, Vaneau drew near the Hotel Romanorum, approaching it on the narrow deserted Canyon Street side, turned quietly into the Canyon Street entrance of it, and went up the stairs. Found the room Spaetz had designated, all right, facing the top of the stairway, and all, just as Spaetz had described, and carrying the Roman numerals on it with which Vaneau himself was familiar, from the several times he'd stopped in that hotel, in previous years. And without knocking—exactly as he'd been invited to do—and he hoped his man *would* be out and that he, Vaneau, could secrete himself in the closet—he quietly opened the door. And there, in the dark room—no, no lights were on at the moment—he saw Spaetz standing, obviously gazing out of the window. He did not move because of the hall light filtering momentarily in. At least, his silhouette against the dark-grey sky hardly changed. Well, Vaneau lost no time. He swept silently, catlike, across that floor—withdrawing, even as he did so, from the practically open bag, the dagger with card attached—and thrust it, with full force—into his victim's back, after which he was out of the room in a trice. Out of the hotel, as well. And that's—that's the story."

"But I—I still just don't get it, Bill," she said. "I can understand—yes—how, after the murder—plainly the murder, as now appears, of a wrong man—the wealthy ex-owner of the dagger never dared speak out, because of the scandal—nor the errant wife, either. Either before her subsequent divorce from Luke Vaneau, nor after. For the same reason—her fine people and family. And thus the murderer was able to go on in life, even to inheriting his paltry $3,000 or so. But what on earth was Ragpicker Joe doing in Mr. Spaetz's room? And how did he get in there? And who removed his body into the mop and broom room? And why did that person remove, from a deck in his pocket, an Ace of Spades? And where was Mr. Spaetz at the time of the murder?"

"Whoa—Tilley!" laughed Bill Chattock. "Them is a lot o' questions! Well, Ragpicker Joe, who, in that story about the old case was also called 'Deafie' and 'Stone-Ear' because of being deaf and—but how thoroughly *did* you read it, darling? Did you read, for instance, how he'd been uncovered, by the work of a detective named DuShane, on the purely dagger phase of things, as a man who at some time in the past had viciously killed a white fellow-ragpicker, and buried his body—yes, I refer to DuShane's own later unearthment of the body of the slain white ragpicker under Joe's tar-paper shack near the dumps, strangled to death, brutally, as was evidenced by a torn bill corner, the said picker having plainly come on a $20 bill. And Joe having once been seen with such a cornerless bill. And atop of all which, Joe's fingerprints, found on the dead man's gold-filled teeth, where Joe had tried futilely to tear them out after the slaying—sa-a-ay, are you letting *me* ramble on to see how much of the story *I* read? If so, I read it all—and as for you, you word-skipper—oh, I see!—you're nodding, eh?—read it all too. Okay, then. Ragpicker Joe was on that particular floor of the Hotel Romanorum that night for the purpose—beyond any doubt whatsoever—of prowling some of the empty rooms later on for nothing more than, say, a roll of good bedclothes, particularly blankets, that he could sell, in the places where he sold his kind of stuff. For Joe, you see, *was* a very, very much small-time operator, to say the least, having even killed his own white friend for but a paltry $20. But as to anybody later removing an Ace of Spades from his deck after any murder, they didn't. For now that we know the *real* facts of the case, we realize that Ragpicker Joe obviously carried a deck of fortune-telling cards from which the awful Death-Card—yes, the Ace of Spades—had been removed by him so that it could *never* come up in the various layouts of the cards. But you ask also where Asoff Spaetz was—at the time of the murder? Well, Asoff Spaetz, at the identical second of the murder, was undoubtedly sitting quietly in his room, patiently awaiting the caller who was going to negotiate with him. Except that, alas for such quaint little things as mix-ups and all, the Hotel Romanorum was today—'today' being then!—using regular Arabian digits on the room doors, instead of the Roman numerals it had used always to carry in other days—such as, for instance, when Luke Vaneau himself had stopped there. And Spaetz had given—and quite correctly!—as his room number, Number Eleven, the '11' that was on his door. And had described it as being at the top of the stairway, facing same. Though the stairway in question actually was—the front stairway of the hotel. And what Luke Vaneau found, at the head of the Canyon Street stairway as he went up it, facing it, was just an unused room in which Ragpicker Joe was waiting till the hotel should quiet down. A room that, not being in use, and connecting with a firescape—yes, the very fire-scape up which Joe had come on his own steam power!—had the word EXIT on the door. Except that the silvered letter E and the silvered letter T of the tacked-on word EXIT had fallen off, long back. Leaving just—the XI thereof. Get it? XI—the Roman numeral—11. The slight modernization, as you might put it, of that hotel, cost Ragpicker Joe his life!"

"Good—heavens!" was all she could say. "EXIT—minus E—minus T— equalling—11! What an amazing problem in—in mathematics *and* spelling combined. And if only, Bill, we knew—you and I—what became of Luke Vaneau, red-handed killer, who killed red-handedly even though he did inadvertently despatch a man who was a black murderer himself—if only we knew what became of Luke Vaneau, we'd know, just you and I, wouldn't we, the whole and complete inside story of a case that's been a 25-year mystery, though could remain so, for all of *me,* for the next thousand years. Unless, of course," she sighed, "Vaneau, having killed once, went from bad to worse. As so often happens."

"I'm so glad," Chattock put in relievedly, "that you feel as you do. I mean—about letting the Past—remain the Past. When the people in it haven't remained at all—the people they were. But insofar as you yourself will some day go to Floyd, Ohio, to see that precious page your papa and mama signed—and you know your father's coding system, and have his 'Codoscope' device—you'll only eventually learn for yourself. What became, I mean, of Luke Vaneau. For, you see, Luke Vaneau was himself the 'Goldie' who, in a dark hour, told your father all. Yes, he was called 'Goldie' because he used to keep his spare money, when he had any, always in gold pieces! But Luke Vaneau was, moreover, a stage name, and your father naturally set down, in his memo, the man's real name. Luke Vaneau is today running a little circus in America's southwest—and his name is—"

"No?" she cried, in utter unbelief. "No?"

"Yes," he said grimly. "Angus MacWhorter is his name. Our secret, now, darling, for all time. Yes?"